Something like a **Hero**

Published by Merlyn's Pen, Inc.
4 King Street
P.O. Box 1058
East Greenwich, Rhode Island 02818-0964

Printed in the United States of America.

These are works of fiction. All characters and events portrayed in this book are fictional, and any resemblance to real people or incidents is purely coincidental.

Cover design by Alan Greco Design.
Cover illustration by Dan Reed.
Section illustrations by Jane O'Conor.
All artwork copyright ©1995.

Library of Congress Cataloging-in-Publication Data

Something like a hero : stories of daring and decision by American teen
    writers /edited by Kathryn Kulpa.
        p.   cm. -- (American teen writer series)
        "All of the short stories in this book originally appeared in Merlyn's
    Pen: The national magazines of student writing"--Acknowledgments.
        Summary: A collection of short stories by teenage writers exploring
    heroism.
        ISBN 1-886427-03-8
        1. Heroes--Juvenile fiction. 2. Short stories, American. 3. Children's
    writings, American. [1. Heroes--Fiction. 2. Short Stories. 3. Children's
    writings.]
    I. Kulpa, Kathryn. II. Series.
PZ5.S6955   1995
[Fic]--dc20   95-10400
                                                                CIP
                                                                AC

99 98 97 96   6 5 4 3 2

Something like a Hero

STORIES OF DARING AND DECISION
BY AMERICAN TEEN WRITERS

Edited by
Kathryn Kulpa

The American Teen Writer Series
Editor: R. James Stahl

Merlyn's Pen, Inc.
East Greenwich, Rhode Island

Acknowledgments

All of the short stories in this book originally appeared in *Merlyn's Pen: The National Magazines of Student Writing.*

The following stories are copyright © by Merlyn's Pen, Inc.: "A Hard Road Home" by Nathan Costa, "A Northern Light" by Andrew Heitzmann, "Junkyard Jaunt" by Robert Jennings, "The Cormorant in My Bathtub" by Brooke Rogers, "Ambush" by Roger Tsai, and "Theft" by Elizabeth Webster.

The following stories are copyright © by the individual authors: "Beneath a Dark Mountain" by Jessica Hekman, "Like One of the Family" by Kathleen Latzoni, "Test of Manhood" by Jonah Steinberg, "A Speck in Infinity" by Julie Wilson, and "It Rained for Stevie" by Jodi Zislis.

The American Teen Writer Series

Young adult literature. What does it mean to you?

Classic titles like *Lord of the Flies* or *Of Mice and Men*—books written by adults, for adult readers, that also are studied extensively in high schools?

Books written for teenagers by adult writers admired by teens—like Gary Paulsen, Norma Klein, Paul Zindel?

Shelves and shelves of popular paperbacks about perfect, untroubled, blemish-free kids?

Titles like *I Was a Teenage Vampire? Lunch Hour of the Living Dead?*

The term "young adult literature" is used to describe a range of exciting literature, but it has never accounted for the stories, poetry, and nonfiction actually written by young adults. African American literature is written by African Americans. Native American stories are penned by Native Americans. The Women's Literature aisle is stocked with books by women. Where are the young adult writers in young adult literature?

Teen authors tell their own stories in *Merlyn's Pen: The National Magazines of Student Writing*. Back in 1985 the magazine began giving young writers a place for their most compelling work. Seeds were planted. Ten years later, The American Teen Writer Series brings us the bountiful, rich fruit of their labors.

Older readers might be tempted to speak of these authors as potential writers, the great talents of tomorrow. We say: Don't. Their talent is alive and present. Their work is here and now.

About the Author Profiles:

The editors of The American Teen Writer Series have decided to reprint the author profiles as they appeared in *Merlyn's Pen* when the authors' works were first published. Our purpose is to reflect the writers' ages, grade levels, and interests at the time they wrote these stories.

Contents

Heroes and Villains

Questing Heroes

Beneath a
Dark Mountain

by JESSICA HEKMAN

PREFACE

In the universe there are an infinite number of worlds
and their suns. In one space of Infinity, circling twin
suns, whirls a planet that embodies all the dreams
of Earth. Across this planet's face roam unicorns, drag-
ons, and elves. Living near a mountain range in the
North are a few humans and rukhs.*

Five decades before this tale, a small tribe of humans called the Alitarril fled the attack of the Onyarx,
a dark race of nightmares: almost human in appearance, but short and round, with snubbed pig's noses
and little black pig's eyes. The humans were driven up
into the mountains and beyond, down to the valley
below, where they were trapped. At the far side of this
valley roared a ceaseless fire.

For a while, doom seemed certain; but when the

---

*Rukhs (pronounced "rocks") are a legendary race of giant birds and
are commonly referred to as rocs. [author's note]

Alitarril entered the valley, they had woken the rukhs
of the mountains. As the Onyarx passed the rukhs in
pursuit of the humans, some regrettable incident occurred; perhaps some rukh was killed. The two races
set upon each other, with the Alitarril waiting for fifty
years as the war raged on, knowing all the while that
whoever won it would come and kill them. And all
the while they cursed their forefathers.

But the rukhs were not content with battling their
lives away. And a cold winter came, forcing the humans to seek fire . . .

The fire grew hotter on Kanya's cheeks as she jogged
along, her red braid swinging with uncharacteristic heav-
iness behind her. She stopped for a moment and set
down the smoothly oiled stick, leaning it carefully against
a rock, to tug at the offending braid. She hated having her hair up, but her mentor, Arlla, had said she
must—to make her way through the Briars . . .

Well, the Briars are long past, thought Kanya defi-
antly, starting to untwine her hair. She felt guilty as
the first strands fell across her cheeks, then frightened
as she thought of the Never-Ending Fire, and bound
it up again hastily. She picked up the torch and ran
her fingers over its smooth surface, feeling the lov-
ingly polished and oiled wood.

I will be sorry when this torch burns, Kanya thought
grimly. She closed her eyes and thought of the red glow
in the sky becoming more brilliantly malevolent by
the night, until it was faintly visible even in the day.
Kanya opened her eyes and stuck the torch in her belt.
She would do this for her people. They needed the

fire because it would be a cold winter in the valley, and none would survive without heat. Fire was the alternative to crossing the mountains en route to warmer lands . . .

Curse the Fathers! thought Kanya as she jogged on again. *Had they no more sense than to be driven through the mountains where the rukhs dwell, and to the very edge of the fire-lands? Were the Onyarx more clever, then, to have outmaneuvered the Fathers?*

Kanya's breath began to come in hot, painful gasps. Her lungs hurt. Still, she smiled to herself at the amusing thought. *An Onyar clever? Never!* She had seen one once as it scouted through the valley. Her father and brother had killed it. Her eyes closed at the bloody memory.

The heat grew so intense that at last Kanya looked up. Just ahead on the horizon was the fire. Its lashing flames snarled and leaped into the air only to fall back hissing at the barrier of trenches built by the Ancients, who had lived in the valley before the coming of the Alitarril. The scalding wind whipped at Kanya and she stopped. She was quite close enough now! She stared at the fire resentfully. Why must it be beautiful? It was deadly and evil. But the red-gold of its flames hummed at her, the Fire-Haired one, she who was said to be the child of fire herself.

Kanya jerked her gaze away. The fire was far too hot for her to get any closer. Not thirty yards away, already it dominated her vision and caused lights to dance in her head when she closed her eyes. This was the part of her journey that she had dreaded. How could she get any fire now? Her people needed fire to live—winter was coming, and with the autumn wind's harsh portent, they knew it would be a bad winter. If the Alitarril had no fire, how would they live?

It's not my fault! Kanya screamed silently. *I was born to this! Why must I get us out? . . . I didn't have to. It was just that we need fire. Arlla thought I should go. It wasn't a vote or anything; she just said I should go, and it seemed like a good idea at the time, so I went. Why didn't I ask someone to come? Why didn't I even tell anyone I was going? I know Arlla influenced my decision; she does that—they say that when she lost the use of her legs she gained greater use of her brain. It's true that she all but rules the village. They also say that, outside of the valley, you needn't grow up so fast. I'm only sixteen . . .*

Kanya sat down with the unlit torch beside her and sighed. If she couldn't get any closer to the fire, how could she get the torch lit so that her people would be warm this winter?

The wind engulfed her, howling like an animal. *Is this how a rukh calls?* she wondered. *I've never seen a rukh. Arlla has . . . that's how she was crippled, they say. I've heard that the rukh broke both her legs, and the tigre Sinnla found her and dragged her back . . . but not in time; she's crippled now and can't walk.*

Kanya thought of Sabre, her own white tigre. The tigres were staunch friends of the Alitarril, unlike the rukhs, who lived in the upper reaches of the mountains above the Onyarx. Rukhs were unpredictable, and surely warlike to have fought the Onyarx for fifty years . . . Kanya closed her eyes again, then opened them and whispered: "May I never see a rukh in my lifetime!" The slowly spoken words died on the whistling wind.

The wind howled again, and a glowing spark flew toward Kanya. *What luck!* she thought, running forward. The spark caught a bush and blazed up. It was, in an instant, too hot to approach. Kanya bit her lip and edged closer. The heat flamed on her bare face and she closed her eyes, shielding them behind an up-flung arm. Kanya grimaced and thought, *I have to do this* . . . But the fire was laughing at her, and she was still so far away!

She crept closer, intent on the nearest spark. The world began to swim with the omnipotent heat, and, staggering backward, she finally thought: *It's not worth it.* She thought about giving up just as a shadow crossed the sky.

Allin circled lower, watching the girl with the long, loose braid that was so red as to be nearly vermilion. *She'll never make it*, he thought, wondering why she seemed so intent on getting herself scorched. He'd seen her fight her way through the thick brambles commonly called the Briars, and had considered offering her a ride back. She was very small, and he liked her spirit. Allin glided lower still as the breeze carrying him died. He watched intently as the girl again crept closer—closer—*why didn't she give up?* With a sudden small sigh, barely audible even to Allin's sharp ears, she sank to the ground.

The rukh swooped down next to her, thinking, *Well, she's done it now.* He beat his wings gently, fanning the fire back, managed to take off again, and, as he hovered above her, picked her up in his talons. It seemed to him that she was very light, barely heavier than one of his own feathers. He glided up higher.

"Let's see," Allin murmured in his strange, grating

language. "She comes from that little village to the north . . ."

Kanya shifted, then abruptly awoke and sat up. Her older sister, Anya, was watching her closely.

Kanya batted Anya's hand away from her forehead. "I'm fine and I *don't* have a fever. Let me be! How'd I get back here?"

"Allin. He's the rukh that brought you back not even an hour ago. He set you down in the middle of the village and has been trying to make us trust him ever since. We've decided that he's trustworthy." Anya hesitated; it seemed that the rukh was still not *absolutely* trusted.

"*A rukh?* Rukhs are enemies!"

Anya shrugged. "Not Allin, it seems. Well, I guess you can get up now if you want to see him."

Kanya promptly got out of bed and pulled on some clothes with childish impatience.

"Kanya?" The voice was very deep and heavily accented, barely recognizable. "Anya, is she conscious? Send her out." The rukh's voice was harsh and forced, as though he were spitting out the unfamiliar words. He stressed the first syllable of every word, whether it ought to have been stressed or not. This was a habit that Kanya soon found irritating.

Kanya tied a band around her head to keep her long, loose hair out of her eyes and stalked out, furious with this Allin rukh for calling her out. But when she saw him she froze. He was gigantic! Looking down at her from a considerable distance, he appeared at least forty feet tall. Kanya regarded him with a touch more respect.

"I want to talk to you," said Allin. "I've spoken to your village already."

Kanya looked around desperately, feeling cornered. Arlla was slumped in her chair, near Allin, grinning at Kanya from ear to ear. Sinnla and Sabre were beside her. She trotted over to stand between the two tigres and nodded at Allin, her hand resting lightly on Sabre's head.

"We rukhs have been your friends," began Allin thickly. "But as you have feared us, we too have feared you. I have spoken to my people on behalf of the Al—Altari—on behalf of your village, and the rukhs agreed that if I spoke with you they might . . . help.

"We fight a common enemy. With fire, we can trap the Onyarx, then cross the fire—your people on the backs of my people—to safety. Come with me. You seem to know the dangers of the fire; you have experience."

Kanya watched the rukh carefully, especially his fiery black eyes. At last she nodded. "I will help you because my kinspeople have consented. But I don't understand."

The rukh nodded briefly. "Do you know that the Onyarx are as afraid of fire as your people? They live far from it, and when they burn campfires they are always carefully controlled. If we place a raging fire at Darrs's two exits, they will be trapped."

Kanya frowned. "It's a mountain. Exits?"

"A very steep mountain. There are only two slender passes which slope gently enough to allow exit.

"I will take you now. Your fallen torch awaits you by the fire," said the rukh. He looked down at Kanya.

"Is there anything you want to bring?"

"Yes. A cloak." Anya materialized behind her sister with a long gray one, and Kanya pulled it over her shoulders and fastened it securely.

"I think the comfortable place for you to ride would be on my back," the rukh continued, "but my feathers are very smooth and you might slip. It would be best if I carried you as I did when I returned you home."

"Excuse me?" muttered Kanya, watching suspiciously as the huge bird lifted its wings. He walked awkwardly away, until he was a little way beyond the village center. Kanya scrambled to follow him.

Allin brought his wings down so forcefully that the wind they generated knocked Kanya flat. Then Allin was in the air, hovering, extending his talons.

"Grab on!" he commanded. Kanya flung an arm over one hooked nail and was promptly lifted up.

As they rose higher into the air, Kanya gritted her teeth and did not look down. Allin curved his talons into a hard seat where Kanya wriggled around in a vain attempt to get comfortable.

"Don't slip out!" the rukh called, hoarsely casting the foreign words to a whipping wind. His voice sounded very high up and far away.

The Briars, nearly a quarter of a mile of thick brambles, passed quickly beneath them. Kanya watched in fascination, remembering the problem they had been for her! Then the fire came into view. It was licking very near the fallen torch already. Kanya frowned.

"It was not that near when I dropped the torch."

"The fire's been growing," replied Allin, rolling his r's slightly. His voice was still thick, but shriller when struck by the heavy wind. "It's this wind," he explained.

"It's pushing the fire closer to the Alitarril. Soon your people will be driven up into the mountains and . . ."

And the Onyarx, thought Kanya sadly. "How am I ever going to get the thing, then?" she yelled into the wind.

"What? The torch? You'll see."

Allin landed a bit nearer to the fire than was comfortable, and Kanya slipped out of his talons to hide behind a leg. "Ow! It's hot!" she complained.

Allin shrugged her off and raised his wings. Kanya flung one arm around his leg and another over her eyes to protect against the heat. His wings began to descend: slowly, then faster, until Kanya could hear the wind whistling around them. She bit her lip in anticipation of being knocked flat again and grabbed Allin's leg more tightly with both arms.

The fire shifted in the resulting wind, while Kanya, sheltered by Allin's leg, managed miraculously to stay up. "Now!" Allin shouted, "while the fire's driven back!"

Kanya ran forward. The heat reflected off her cloak, but she could feel her unprotected cheeks growing red. Grimly she pressed forward.

Kanya heard a faint whooshing sound, which grew louder, and then the wind from Allin's wings knocked her flat again! "Darn," she groaned, face in the dirt. She looked back over her shoulder at Allin with a black glare.

"Run! Hurry!"

Suddenly she realized that she had to get that torch *now!* She charged forward, barely on her feet, and grabbed it. It was blazing hot and burning at one end. She wrapped a corner of her cloak around it and held that. The fire came rushing back, straight at her. She stumbled back, biting her lip. If Allin chose to blow on the fire now, she'd be knocked into it . . .

The heat was infernal. Kanya regained her balance, turned, and ran. Allin's wing twitched and the fire wavered slightly in the wind. She drew closer to the tall bird and, simultaneously, felt the fire drawing nearer to her.

Allin thrust his beak toward her, his eyes urgent. She grabbed it and scrambled up. His head lifted as he took off.

As soon as the bumpy takeoff was over, Kanya slid forward into a position similar to riding a tigre. "Don't speak!" she warned Allin, "or you'll knock me right off!" She patted his beak with a grin. "Thanks," she smiled.

Allin rumbled deep in his chest at the familiarity, but flew on.

They flew right past the village of the Alitarril. Kanya looked back sharply at Allin's eyes. *Can't you see because I'm in the way?* she thought. *There's my village!* But she did not want him to answer her question and knock her off his beak—it was a long way to the ground.

They kept going, straight on, until the mountains loomed ahead. Allin banked and finally landed at the base of a mountain. He lowered his bill to the ground, and Kanya slipped off, glaring at him.

"What are you doing?" she snapped. "There are Onyarx up there. They'll kill me!"

Allin regarded her silently for a moment before speaking. "They might kill me as well. I think that my death is rather more probable—don't you? You can hide." His voice held no malice, only stark fact. Kanya looked at those fiery black eyes and thought: *He's re-*

*ally going to kill himself for his people! And my peo-
ple! I should be willing to die, too. But I'm not!*

"Why are we here?" she asked him curtly, holding
the fiery torch low so that the glare wouldn't obstruct
her line of vision.

He whispered—and it is interesting to hear a rukh
whisper—"We are going to set fire to the base of Darrs
Mountain, and to the world of the Onyarx within it."

His whispering caressed Kanya like a breeze, and
when he said "fire" he rolled his *r* as a true rukh should.
She shivered as he misused one word—"world" instead of "settlement"; it made him seem alien, not the
Allin she had known for—how long? Only a few hours,
but it seemed a year. He looked nervous: every so often he shifted from foot to foot, as Kanya had seen
sparrows do. She had never heard him stumble when
speaking her language, but when she saw the black
pools of flame that should have been eyes, she said
nothing and waited.

"The Onyarx will be trapped as they ought—as
they have trapped us, and you."

"*You* are trapped?" Kanya looked up at the towering rukh, thought of the man-sized Onyar she'd seen
killed, and thought again: *Trapped?*

"The Onyarx do know some little magic," replied
the rukh quietly. "All black. We cannot cross the mountains or the fire. It is a form of—how do you say it?
They hold a curse over us: this is the only mountain
that will ever be our home, and if we go to another
our eggs will have thin shells and will break when we
warm them; food will be scarce and we will grow
sick . . ." He glanced away from her, up at his home.
"Fire," he added, "it is cleansing. It will destroy the

spell. We will escape."

Kanya lifted her torch and said, "We will live, my friend, to take them away from here ourselves."

Allin watched her torch burning low and red, then nodded. He lifted his wings once again beneath the glowing sky, the stars brilliant against the blanket of blackness. He said, "I am accustomed to flying from the heights of cliffs. This is the last time I'll take off from the ground today."

Kanya grabbed his talons and slipped eel-like into them as the rukh lifted her from the ground. They flapped higher, his wings straining, and the mountains were thrown into such stark relief that Kanya shivered again. She was not cold. "I never knew—they look so peaceful from the village."

A few small, carefully contained Onyarx fires glowed in pinpoints on the hillsides. The jagged cliffs reared up sharply, cut and scarred vilely by the roads of the Onyarx. A dark, heavy, putrid smell drifted steadily up, marking the presence of Onyarx. A few caves gutted the hills, empty and lean. Hunger and fear were in the air.

The rukh glided slowly—silently—higher, until the air grew thin and Kanya nearly choked. Then he swerved sharply to one side and landed in a mountain nest.

"Illai?" he called softly. He curled up one leg to safely hide Kanya. A smaller, lighter-colored rukh edged out of the shadows.

"Time?" he rasped, his Alitarril barely recognizable.

"It is." In a barely audible voice Allin said, "This is Illai. He will take you to the base of the mountains to set your fire while I speak to the other rukhs. They will be ready when you return."

Kanya twisted around and stared up at him: *Must I go with a strange rukh?*

"Illai is to be trusted. He is smaller and lighter than I, and not as opinionated as some. I am the only one who can sway the other rukhs; I did do one small thing for them that will be remembered, I think. Now go. I do not trust the Onyarx; they are cunning and therefore good at hiding about our aeries at night."

Kanya was gently transferred to Illai, who glided off the mountain. Kanya tried to burn neither him nor herself with her torch and thought: *I never knew Allin was so big until I saw Illai! These talons are small!*

They crossed the mountains at a high speed, Illai straining to fly as fast as he could. "There, little one," he told her in an accent so thick as to be barely understandable. "Set red heat about these!"

The bushes were parched from lack of water and had never seen fire in their lives. Kanya struck about her with the torch so that hot flames sprang up. Illai fanned them gently back, in a circle around the base of the mountain. Kanya ran ever faster, her feet aching, trying to beat time—she must hurry before she was discovered . . . Illai was always behind her, wings fanning gently, carefully forcing the fire to stay where they wanted it, his bill gouging trenches to guide the fire in a close circle around the small mountain's base. Soon the rukh began to pull up bracken and set it in bare places, so that the fire caught at it and roared hungrily, blazing up.

"Good," he said at last, taking her cloak abruptly in his beak and lifting her up into the air. Kanya, gasping for breath, reached up and hung on to his beak.

They flew only about a quarter of a mile before Illai said, placing her gently on the ground, "More red heat must set here. Heat on both sides—surround!"

Kanya ran, pressing the torch deep into the dry branches. Her hands were scraped from twigs and thorns and her arms ached. Faster! She must keep on outrunning the hungry fire . . .

"Enough. Will burn on its own," said Illai at last. "Go back."

Gratefully, Kanya grabbed the bill he offered her. He lifted her up over his shoulder and set her gently down on his back.

"Easy now . . . feathers slippery."

"Slippery and big as mallee leaves," muttered Kanya, thinking of the six-foot leaves of a particular tree. Illai chuckled, beating his way laboriously up into the air.

The pointed cliff rose up in front of them. As soon as they landed, Kanya tumbled off Illai and ran to Allin. He was speaking earnestly with a big bird in his own language, but turned at Kanya's shout. Lowering his beak he said, "Hush, little one. You are back sound?"

Safe and sound, Kanya thought, but she only nodded and touched his beak in greeting. Allin tried to return her smile—or so it seemed—but his beak could not twist up into a grin like hers, and he shrugged.

"This is Miunatin," he announced, "the Mother. Our leader. I saved her life from an Onyar when her wing was wounded—thus I do have some little influence over our people. They will come. And the fire—?" He broke off, looking back at the base of the mountain. Already smoke was rising.

"Good, little one. Now, Illai, you may come; we go to set a fire to the settlement at Darrs Mountain."

Kanya raised her torch. It was burning low. "We must hurry."

The other rukhs watched as the trio glided gently off the mountain. Kanya swallowed convulsively as they drifted lower, nearer to the Onyarx, bane of the Alitarril, at Darrs . . .

They landed on a ledge a little beyond the fort. Kanya's eyes instantly focused on the huge iron gates and the scattered huts within. A few Onyarx guards stood, only half-vigilant, at Darrs's entrance. Kanya could see that the village was fairly open, but deeply shadowed. And the huts would burn nicely.

"Go, quickly," hissed Allin. "I'll distract them." Kanya slipped off (her heart was in her mouth, so she swallowed it) and ran, unobserved, toward Darrs's gates.

Allin jumped off the ledge with a shriek and a howl, bringing Darrs's Onyarx running. He made a great commotion on the ground, flapping his wing as if it were wounded.

"Hurry!" called Illai, as Kanya charged past the distracted guards and through the gates. He motioned to the spears and arrows that the Onyarx were gathering. "Death," said the young rukh.

Not Allin—he could never die, thought Kanya.

It was very dark, and she ran in the shadows and with the shadows. The stink of the piggish Onyarx filled her nose and stomach; she gagged. They were all over, like maggots. Kanya remembered—just in time—to shield the torch's glow with her body. Perhaps, hunkered over like this, she would appear to be an Onyar—at least, to the bleary eyes of an Onyar . . . *Quickly now, before they see the gleam of the torch!*

Kanya began setting the fire, praying that the torch

would last just a moment longer. Soon the blaze was crackling wildly, and Onyarx were running toward her.

Abandoning the torch to the fire, Kanya ran an obstacle course around the clumsy creatures. Ahead were the gates! Allin, beyond, raised his head in surprise when he saw her; Illai started forward but was too far away. She was almost to the gates when panic set in and the world began to spin. She stumbled . . .

A heavy hand clamped down on her shoulder and whipped her around. She stared into the leering face of an Onyar.

Meanwhile, Allin's "wounded" wing had become a sweeping arc, knocking down Onyarx in a huge semicircle around him. He had long since given up the game of being wounded and was fighting for his life. Two arrows, mere pins to him, were embedded in his wings. He saw the Onyar draw his knife, ready for a quick kill, and tried to run to Kanya's aid. But the rukh's talons were not made for running and he had to hop awkwardly, calling Illai to help him.

Luckily the Onyar did not seem inclined toward a quick kill, and he was too absorbed in Kanya to notice the quiet rukh or the horrified screams of his people. As the knife cut her arm, Illai's beak descended and swung sideways, knocking the Onyar away.

The creature was flung fifteen feet and landed hard, but he was tough as iron and sat up only a little dizzily. When he saw Kanya getting away, he grabbed a spear, drew it back and aimed carefully for a one-chance throw.

Allin beat his wings, trying unsuccessfully to take off. Wings half-extended, he hopped forward for a running start, Kanya hanging on to one thick leg.

Suddenly there was a *thunk* above her. Kanya looked up to see Allin's belly shudder, then right itself.

"I'm fine," the rukh called. "But you may have to ride Illai out . . ." His voice was faint.

Kanya closed her eyes against the hard world and the heat as Allin finally got beyond the gates. With one last surge of Rukhian strength, he fairly tossed her to Illai, and in an instant Kanya and Illai were in the air. Kanya peeked out from her cradle in Illai's legs and looked down at Allin, who was still trying to take off.

The big rukh was flapping his wings desperately, hordes of Onyarx closing in. Only now could Kanya see the hindering spear embedded to its butt in his wing. She drew in her breath as another spear sank into his belly. Now the Onyarx were circling him, throwing spear after spear. At last the great rukh turned away and sank down near the fire. He never twitched.

"Illai!" screamed Kanya. "They're killing him! Go back! Save him!"

"Is already dead," replied Illai.

"But he was my *friend*," cried Kanya.

"Was my father," snapped Illai, his words very guttural and forced.

Kanya had thought that Allin would never die. Now he was dead. He would never see the freedom he had given his life for. Kanya curled up and sobbed.

The Alitarril and the rukhs gathered swiftly and quietly in the dark, hardly speaking. Kanya sat outside her house with her friend Sabre pressed up against her in feline silence. Sabre fended off all the Alitarril who wished to thank Kanya, keeping her alone as she wished to be.

Illai whispered something to Miunatin, and she nodded. "It is time to fly," Illai announced, "over the fire to a new land."

The Alitarril were already climbing awkwardly onto some birds, lugging their belongings up behind them. Kanya stared up at Illai. "Can't I just stay?" she asked.

"Our people are alike. Feel much the same," replied Illai. "But life worth living, will find, little one. I take comfort in that have you."

His eyes, very cautious now, were hard and dark as he said this, the light fire of life gone; it was a chance he was taking. Kanya looked up into those black jewels—how unlike Allin's fiery eyes!—and nodded her tear-streaked face. Illai lowered his beak and carefully picked up Sabre, to set him on his dark back. Then he offered his bill to Kanya.

Kanya bit her lip and allowed herself to be raised up.

"Now we go!" called Illai, and the rukhs and Alitarril all flew up high over the fire, into the rosy sunrise.

ABOUT THE AUTHOR

Jessica Hekman lives in Claremont, California, where she attends the ninth grade at Vivian Webb School. "Beneath a Dark Mountain," mostly written in the eighth grade at Pioneer Junior High School, in Upland, won recognition in the Promising Young Writers Program sponsored by the National Council of Teachers of English.

Junkyard Jaunt

by ROBERT JENNINGS

The full moon illuminated the woods, lighting the way as Harvey Thiggle and Ray Pherberrey vainly tried to find civilization. So far, no luck. No lights, no houses, no highways, nothing. Just trees, trees, and more trees, as far as the eye could see. Harvey was getting sick of looking at them. It was all he'd been doing for the past two hours, ever since Super Boy Scout Ray figured out that they'd been following a helicopter instead of the North Star.

Once again, Harvey's mind turned to the events that had made them lose their way. Halloween night. Trick-or-treating. Ray screaming rude words at a large group of high school seniors. Ray hauling butt into the woods. Harvey following him. Realizing that they weren't being chased anymore. Realizing that they were hopelessly lost. "I wanna go home," Harvey muttered.

"Yeah, Harv, me too. But at the moment, going home isn't an option. C'mon, let's get truckin'." Ray trudged onward.

Harvey followed suit, rubbing his growling stomach and cursing his aching feet. The aging Nikes he wore didn't make the best hiking shoes. If it weren't for Ray cussing out the big kids, Harvey would be home now. He didn't know what was wrong with Ray. Ray always tried to emulate the can-do bravery of his Green Beret father. That would have been A-OK if Harvey didn't have to play the role of enlisted man to Ray's platoon commander fantasy.

Suddenly, the Fearless Leader exclaimed, "Cool! Check it out!"

Instantly, Harvey quit slouching and sped up. "What? Do you see houses?"

Ray pointed straight ahead. "A junkyard! Look at all those cars!"

Harv trotted up beside him and scowled. The place was deserted. "That's nice. A junkyard. Gee, now all we have to do is choose a car and zip on home."

Ray didn't hear him. He took off for the huge compound, calling back, "Come on! Maybe there's a security guard or someone who can help us!"

"Yeah, and maybe that security guard will blow our heads off for trespassing!" Although Harvey knew it wasn't smart, he wriggled through a hole in the chain-link fence after Ray. The way things looked, he had no choice. It was either go through, or stay on the outside, alone in the dark woods. Staying outside was doubtlessly safer, but Harvey's conscience wouldn't let him stand by while a turkey like Ray ran around unsupervised on somebody else's property.

As soon as he was through, a frightening thought hit him like a speeding bus. "Ray? What if this place has guard dogs? You know, like Dobermans? I don't think we should be here."

Ray picked up a length of pipe, hefting it up in his right hand. "If they have Dobermans, we'll just have to . . ." He swung the pipe, smashing a soda bottle to pieces on the ground, "deal with them accordingly." He picked up a tire iron out of a scrap heap and threw it to his companion.

Harvey turned the cold iron over in his hands, knowing how useless it was. If any big dogs attacked, he didn't plan to wait for them to get close enough to bash. No, if anything barked, he'd be skedaddling back to that hole in the fence! Even so, he tucked it in the belt of his burglar costume for moral support.

CREEAAK! The rusted door of a 1987 Plymouth Reliant screeched as Ray forced it open and climbed inside.

"Hey, we're supposed to be looking for someone to help us!"

From inside the car, Ray answered, "That's why you never get dates, Harv. You worry too much. Have some fun, man! You're never gonna get to raid a junk-yard at night again, so take the chance now! There's a ton of treasures to be found! You can run on ahead and look for help like a good little boy, but I'm looking for money. I know for a fact that people leave all kinds of change in these . . . aha! Here's a quarter! I wonder what's under the seat."

Harvey shivered. He had a pretty good idea of what might be under the seat. A hibernating snake, that's what. Or worse, a wide-awake snake that was looking for a bedtime snack. God, how reckless Ray was! Living in a military family had taken its toll on his sanity. Harvey wondered if all Army children were like that.

Meanwhile, Ray tired of the Plymouth. He moved on to a boxy early '80s Buick Skylark. Harvey leaned against the hood and tried to think of something to say that would bring Ray to his senses. All of a sudden, the car's two headlights came to life and lit up the entire area in front of it. "Awesome!" Ray squealed happily. "The battery's still good! Who says American cars aren't built to last?"

"Ray, turn those off! If there's anybody here and they see you playing with their stuff . . ."

As always, Ray wasn't listening. "Hmmm. I wonder if the horn—"

"NO!" Harvey cried, but it was too late. Ray brought his fist down in a hard, hammerlike motion, and an ear-piercing *HONNNNNK!* shattered the silence of the junkyard. Amused, Ray did it again, laughing like a lunatic. *HONNNK!*

"STOP!"

HONNNNNNNK! "Heeheehee!"

"YOU TURKEY!" Harvey, high on adrenaline, looked toward the hole in the fence.

"Aw, come on, Harv," Ray laughed, "don't be so boring. I'm just having a little fun. If I thought there was anybody here, I wouldn't . . . hooo, boy!" Ray didn't quite understand what his friend was getting at until a light came on in a previously invisible house way over on the other side of the junkyard, and the sound of a screen door banging open reached his ears. Perceiving a problem, he took off after his fleeing friend.

Like a pair of missiles, they shot straight toward the hole and safety. The sharp crack of a .22 rang out, hitting home inches from Harvey's foot. He screamed, changed his course, and ran away from the hole, finally ducking behind a 1973 Chevy Impala. Ray fell down beside him. "There's somebody here!"

Harvey felt like hitting him. "Duh! I can see that! And he's trying to kill us! He almost blew my foot off! I could have been killed!"

"This changes everything," Ray said.

"We're going to die here."

"Harv, don't blow a gasket. You don't see me getting all scared, do you?"

A single look at Ray's face gave Harvey the answer to that one: Yes. Even in the shadows cast by the mammoth Impala, Ray's pale face was plainly visible, and Harv could see sweat beading his brow in spite of the cold. Ray wiped off the sweat and pursed his lips. "Yeah, this is gonna take some finesse."

The gun fired twice more, putting out one of the Skylark's headlights twenty feet away. Ray's Adam's apple bobbed as he peered over the Texas-sized hood. "He must be pretty close. How else would he know what to shoot at?"

"Because YOU left those stupid high beams on, that's why! What were you thinking when you did that? No, on second thought, why WEREN'T you thinking?"

Ray didn't answer. He appeared to be in deep thought (for once). Harvey thought he must be blanking out when suddenly his eyes lit up. "Hey! I think I know where we are now! Crazy Jim's Auto Salvage! On Mainline Boulevard! All we have to do is get to the gate, run a mile down the road, and we're home free. Easy, huh?"

CRACK! CRACK! The last headlamp went out, making the moon the only source of light. Harv closed his eyes tightly. It was dark, but that gunman already had an idea of where they were. Oh, man. He didn't feel so good. Conflicting reactions inside his head told him to run, hide, surrender, get down, and crawl back to the fence (if he could remember where it is). He knew this feeling. *Panic.* The feeling that overcame him when the seniors were chasing him down the road, threatening his life. Mortal fear! It was only starting, but it was there. Any minute now, the reality of this situation would smack him full force. Unlike Ray. Harv kicked the fear aside as best he could. He couldn't let Ray see the thin thread that held him together. "You forgot a few details, friend," he said, trying to sound calm. "First, the gate will be locked. Second, we have to pass the house to get to the gate. Third, we have to pass through a quarter mile of Hell to get to the house. Fourth, we have to evade Crazy What's-his-name and his gun to get through the quarter mile of Hell!"

"Not a problem. The lock's gonna be a piece of cake. We can jump the fence, or bust it with a tire iron. And getting by this guy . . . That's easier than flunking a math test. I've seen this old loon before. They call him Crazy Jim. He's at least sixty, he's a big fat slob, and he has more whiskey in him than a Jack Daniels factory. Even YOU could escape from an old fat drunk dude, even if he does have a gun. Don't get so panicky. Relax, chill out."

"A guy whose first name is Crazy is shooting at me—and you're telling me to chill? You're crazier than HE is!"

"This is child's play. My dad put up with machine guns and grenade launchers blasting away at him in 'Nam. Just follow my orders, let me do the worrying, and this will become a pleasant memory. First order: run now, whine later." Ray hunched over and ran a good twelve feet before gunfire made him take cover again. Not wanting to get separated, Harvey scrambled over to him, crawled into the nearest open car, and balled up in the back seat. He wasn't giving in to the panic, but he strongly believed in Grandpa's old saying: "When the going gets tough, the intelligent seek shelter." Or as Ray's dad would pithily say, "If somebody shoots at you, take cover."

Ray grabbed his arm and pulled him out, disgusted. "Don't you do this, don't you dare wuss out on me now! Get on your feet! You think I want to get captured? Come on!"

"But he'll murder me . . ."

"If you'd quit squawking like a baby, maybe he'd have nothing to home in on! I'm gonna run over to that Gran Torino over there and keep an eye on Crazy Jim. You stay here and get your thoughts together." Ray crept along the row of cars, tripped on a driveshaft, and went sprawling on his face. The noise attracted another burst of gunfire. Bullets shattered the Ford Gran Torino's windshield, but Ray kept his cool. He got up, motioning for Harvey to come after him.

As they made their way through the confusing maze of cars and trucks, Harvey heard a noise, a noise that scared him as much as the bullets did. Not far away, the sound of rattling cans and a body hitting the ground signified Jim's presence. Jim spewed cuss words, slurring them so badly that Harv could barely tell what they were. The man was drunk, and although Harv was no rocket scientist, he knew exactly what this meant. Yes, alcohol dulls people's senses, including the sense of right and wrong. If Jim got close enough, he wouldn't shoot to scare, or shoot to wound and take to the police. He was an angry wino, and he would shoot to kill.

Harv tried to ignore the churning acid in his stomach and the ulcer he knew was forming that very minute. He wasn't used to life like this. The most dangerous experience he'd ever had was walking across the street without looking both ways.

They stopped for rest, taking cover in a windowless Dodge minivan. The vehicle's interior was entirely bare, save a single tan velour driver's seat. The back was empty and fire-blackened, but it would do. While Ray caught his breath, Harvey wiped tears from his eyes and looked about. No sign of Jim. Maybe he'd passed out somewhere. The place looked dead: cars lined up in rows, some stacked up on each other; motorcycles, parts, garbage strewn all over; rats scurrying here and there. The light cast by the moon gave it an eerie horror-story quality, doing nothing to improve Harv's mood. Harv blew his nose into the monogrammed handkerchief he kept in his right pocket and stared at a huge Mack truck close by. A bird was perched on the roof. Suddenly, it took to the air and fluttered off into the night. The sound of its beating wings gave Crazy Jim a new target. He fired six times in the truck's general direction.

He missed the bird.

He hit the truck. And its gas tank.

BOOOOOOOOOOOOOM!

The shock wave tipped the minivan over on its side, hurling Harvey and Ray against the opposite wall. The sharp bang Harvey's head received from the sliding side door clarified everything: he was an intelligent human being. And intelligent human beings, when shot at, either shoot back or hide. Since Harvey had no gun, the only thing he could do was cover his head and hide. Hide well. Hide long. Hide forever, if possible. Don't let any moron like Ray drag you out into the line of fire. Be a wuss! Remember, Harv, a wuss lives a heck of a lot longer than a hero.

Ray sat up, groaning. "I think I'm OK. Bruised shoulder, my tailbone's no good, and I think I broke my left pinkie. I can still run, though. Harv, you OK? No broken bones? Good. Let's go. He'll be here any minute!"

Harvey roly-polied on the floor of the van, tucking his head between his knees. "I know! That's why I am shutting up and laying low! If you'll quit babbling your fool head off, maybe he won't find us!"

Ray kicked open the back door, then kicked Harvey as well. Harv rolled out, hitting the cold ground. "You wanna go to jail?" Ray hissed. "Huh? Is that it? You wanna go to jail? That's exactly what's gonna happen if you stay here. If that sick rat doesn't blow your head off, he'll call in the cops, and don't you think for a second that any judge will listen to your story. Your nerd butt was on someone else's property unlawfully, bud! You're guilty as hell, and hiding won't change it!"

Harvey tried to crawl back in. "If he can't find me, he can't bust me. Now, if you had an ounce of sense . . ."

Ray dragged him out again. "Listen, if you want to throw yourself at the mercy of Crazy Jim and the U.S. court system, that's peachy keen with me, but I'm leaving. If you live through it, I hope you never get drafted!"

Ray blinked, looked backwards once, then spoke again. His voice was lowered now, composed but dead serious. "Listen closely. Did you hear something? That's Crazy Jim. Hear him stumble? Hear him curse? He's going to kill you if he finds you, and he's pretty damn close to it. I'd say he's fifty yards away, tops. I can see the barrel of his rifle pointing in the air. I'm gonna give you one last chance. If you crawl back in, I'm not going to drag you out again."

"I . . . I . . ." Harvey didn't know what to say. Make a run for safety with Ray the Wacko Turkey, or spend the night alone in a reeking minivan and hope Crazy Jim sobered up some before finding him. Neither choice looked good, and time was running out.

CRACK! CRACK! CRACK! Three .22 caliber bullets whizzed overhead, making up Harvey's mind for him. "I know where y'all is! I's gonna *BUUUURRRRRRRRP* kill y'all! Ain't nobody who gets away with crossin' Jim!"

"I'm with you," Harvey said. He ignored the screaming bump on his head and jumped to his feet. Harvey S. Thiggle would hide from his problems no more. Henceforth, he would RUN from them! He ran for his life, ran fast, ran scared. More shots cracked the night air, but that didn't slow him. The entrance was in sight. Fifty yards . . . forty-nine . . . forty-eight . . .

Ray swerved and hit the deck beside the remains of a Studebaker Commander. "What are you doing?" Harvey croaked, his voice brimming with fear. "You said we had to run! He's on our tails! We're gonna die!" He looked over his shoulder. There was Jim, not six car-lengths behind them, trying to stuff bullets into his .22. Harvey could see the moonlight glinting off the brass shells that fell out of his shaking hands onto the ground.

"See that gate?" Ray whispered. "It's got a lock, and I lost my tire iron. We'll have to change our plans. We'll go over the fence . . . you CAN climb a fence, can't you?"

Harvey looked at the ground.

"Can't you?"

He shook his head.

"Ahh, this is just great! I can't break the lock! Holy Sh—"

"I'S GONNA GREASE Y'ALL . . . OUCH!" Harvey looked back and saw Jim get up and fall on his face, his left foot planted in a bald-headed tire.

Harv pulled the tire iron out of his belt. "I can crack that lock."

"It takes you six swings with a fly swatter to kill a mosquito, Harv, so don't expect me to wait up. You can try to bust that lock, but I'm jumping the fence. Adiós, amigo!" Ray made a dash for it. Seconds later, he was halfway up.

As Ray dropped over the side, Harvey struck the rusty Yale lock repeatedly. It wasn't breaking! Oh, God! Harv saw Jim stepping over the motorcycle wreck Ray had jumped not moments before. Crazy Jim was within point-blank range. Two shots rang out, and with all his might, Harvey gave it one last try . . .

The two bullets hit home. The tire iron jerked out of his hands, and at the same time, sparks flew from the lock, searing Harvey's hands.

"Ha! Hold 'er right there, you cotton-pickin' crim'-nal!"

A hand gripped his wrist and yanked violently. Harvey

cried out as Ray pulled him through the gate. Harv turned to see Jim, fifteen feet away, point the gun, pull the trigger, and howl with frustration when the rifle clicked empty. Ray laughed, and shouted, "Hey, Jim! Your aim stinks! My grandma shoots better than you, and she's dead!"

The fat, wrinkled, dirty man dropped his rifle and shook his fist. "I'll sic the law on y'all! Just wait 'n' see!" He took a staggering step toward them, then plopped down on his rump.

"Yeah, right, you hick! I bet you don't even have a phone!"

This time, it was Harvey who did the pulling. He grabbed the sleeve of Ray's Halloween costume and urged him onward. "We'll give him a crank phone call someday. Let's just get out of here before he reloads that .22!"

Ray talked almost the whole way home. "Wasn't that cool? Remember this day, Harv. I know I will! It was kind of fun, when you think about it. Sort of like 'Mission Impossible.' You know what? I liked it. I want more. Back there, that was baby stuff."

When they passed a streetlight, Harvey took note of a large wet stain in the pants of Ray's soldier uniform, but he said nothing.

Harvey S. Thiggle: Harvey got home at 11:24 P.M., greeting his shocked parents at the door as they spoke to the police. His mother fainted with relief. Mr. Thiggle, however, was less than happy. He told Harvey that next time he stayed out that late without calling, it would be best not to come home at all. Harvey's sentence: one month's grounding; no Twinkies for a month; no Nintendo for three weeks; no TV for two weeks; no talking on the phone for one week. In addition, he had to give up his room to his nine-year-old cousin Ursula when she came to visit.

Raymond Pherberrey: When Ray got home at 11:25 P.M., his mother was under sedation. Lt. Col. Richard Pherberrey was wide awake. Ray's sentence: five hundred pushups, five hundred sit-ups, thirty laps around the house, and one hundred ninety-pound bench presses (on the spot, to be completed under the watchful eye of Lt. Col. Pherberrey, all before Ray went to bed). Ray was also forced to wash his neighbor's mobile home for free, and write a letter of apology to his mother.

Neither of the boys went trick-or-treating again.

ABOUT THE AUTHOR

Robert Jennings lives in Norfolk, Virginia, where he attends Maury High School. He wrote this story while in the tenth grade. He reports: "I enjoy building replicas of muzzle-loading weapons, handling guns of any kind, and someday hope to take up hang-gliding—a wee bit impractical on a budget like mine." A junkyard enthusiast, Mr. Jennings and some of his friends were recently chased out of one by "some lady on a bulldozer."

Test of Manhood

by JONAH STEINBERG

Yaaaii!"
"Never like that! You'll never have it unless you put the right feeling into your blows."

Embarrassed, Rorik Glowlimn turned to face the open door in which the massive figure of Urik Ironarm stood. Rorik had not expected to be watched and the sly warrior, in his usual fashion, had managed to bring his huge, muscular body into the room without making the slightest noise.

Rorik was a young lad of eighteen, the only son of a rich and honored armorer who had left him all his wealth and a magical sword in hopes that Rorik would one day become a warrior. Nothing, however, was further from young Rorik's mind than the idea of becoming a sword wielder of any sort, let alone a warrior. Rorik was a shy, timid lad who could not stand the thought of killing any living creature, especially creatures with any sort of advanced intelligence, and such was a warrior's job.

Now that I have written this far, it is necessary to explain the incident described and to tell you how this story happened to come to my attention.

On a recent scientific trip I came across a strange gem which I kept, hoping to mount it in a ring. Much to my surprise, when I held the gem up to the light to examine it, a page of rune-like writing about a meter large was projected onto the wall behind me. In turning the gem around, I found that every facet projected another page of the runes. Needless to say, I was interested in the writings and, with the help of several natives of the area, I began translating them.

This is the story of the gem. Of course some of the details were not included in the gem, so I have added my own bits and pieces to the story to convey my picture of what happened, Lord knows how many thousands of years ago, when a civilization, of which this gem-told story is the only trace, existed.

The civilization in which Rorik lived was like the type of world we hear about in fairy tales. Rorik's people had learned to master a power which can only be described as magic. This magic existed in the very stone of the mountain on which the people lived; it was in plants and animals as well, and the people referred to it as Earth's Will. Through the mastering of Earth's Will by devout believers, called simply Earth Workers, certain plants and animals could be used in healing or in making magic potions for many purposes, and certain metals could be fashioned into magical weapons, but these were rare. Few people possessed such weapons.

Rorik was one of the lucky ones.

Rorik himself, at the moment when we left him, was not feeling very lucky; in fact, he was wishing that the sword had never come into his life. As he was now considered a man, it was time, by tradition, for him to go on a quest with an experienced swordsman to prove his manhood. This quest, of course, involved killing some creature of one sort or another and, as Rorik possessed a magical sword, it was sure to be a difficult quest. And what lad of eighteen in his right mind would refuse his quest and bring shame to his family, especially if he owned a sword fashioned of the rarest and most powerful magical metals? The problem was that Rorik had not been able to master the sword's magic. To him, the sword was just a dead piece of ornamental metal.

"If your father," said Urik Ironarm, eyeing scratches that the boy in his careless swordplay had made on the walls, "could see what you do with the sword that he had the power to wield but could not because of his maimed arm, I swear he would turn over in his grave. A magical sword should be treated with respect, not swung around like a club! Why, every swing you take with that sword is worth gold. I would give my right eye for a sword like that!"

"Then take it," said Rorik, on the verge of tears. It was true, he thought: who was he to touch a magical sword? He who could not stand the thought of killing anything. He was a coward, he thought, and he knew it.

"Bah!" grumbled Urik as he strode purposefully

out of the room.

Urik Ironarm was by far the most feared and respected of all the warriors on the mountain. He was an extremely large and powerful man, but he was also very intelligent and cunning as a fox. He spoke sparingly, and only when he felt strongly about something. His usual attire consisted of fur boots, pants made of tough leather, a belt pierced with sharp studs from which a giant sword showing traces of many encounters hung, a shirt made of fine but tough chain mail, and a helmet from which two tufts of feathers protruded like horns. The most remarkable thing about Urik Ironarm was his age; he was 213 years old. He had achieved this incredible age with the help of a gem which hung from a chain around his neck. This gem was cut from the very heart of the mountain and had the power of giving its wearer an almost eternal life. Without the gem Urik supposed he could live about a day before he died.

Urik had been a friend of Rorik's father, who died when Rorik was still a baby, and he had promised Rorik's father that he would take some time from his immense lifetime to guide Rorik on his first quest. For Rorik, this in itself was an honor—an honor he felt he did not deserve. In addition, it made other lads of Rorik's age terribly jealous—of Rorik's wealth, of his sword, and of his guide. There were many boys Rorik believed to be more deserving of these honors than himself. This only added to his humiliation.

There was nothing Rorik could do except pack and prepare for the quest, and hope and pray that the Council of Elders would select an easy quest for him.

The next day, the day before he was to leave on his

adventure, Rorik dressed in his best clothes. He put on his belt with the sheath in which his beautiful sword lay and made his way to the House of Law, where the Council of Elders sat, to hear what his task was to be. The House of Law was in the center of Rorik's mountain village. It was a huge, tall, circular building constructed of whole trunks of tall trees. It had one door and no windows. The only light came through the cracks between the tree trunks. As Rorik entered, he could barely make out the seven figures sitting on a semicircular bench. Beside the bench and to the right stood a massive figure who could only be one man— Urik Ironarm.

The proclaiming of the task was not as long as Rorik thought it would be. One of the elders stood up and said solemnly, "Rorik Glowlimn, son of Durin Glowlimn, your task, to be performed before the next full moon, is . . ." Rorik inhaled deeply and loudly and thought he caught a sharp glance from Urik at the other end of the room, ". . . to kill the sandgorgon of Eagle Peak."

Rorik nearly collapsed in shock. He had expected a hard task: to kill several hill bears or some other animal which would require more skill than he had; but to kill a sandgorgon, let alone the sandgorgon of Eagle Peak, was not only a hard task—it was impossible.

For years the village had been under almost constant attack by one sandgorgon after another, and always a group of warriors had gone out and killed it. The sandgorgon of Eagle Peak was another matter. This sandgorgon had eluded its attackers, and not even

Urik Ironarm could track it down, though he had come close to killing it before it ran from him.

Rorik had never seen a sandgorgon. No boy under eighteen had. Rorik, as other boys his age, had always gone into the shelter of a cave with the women. From the tales that Rorik had heard, he knew sandgorgons to be horrible, lizard-like creatures, and he had always hoped that he should never have to see one, let alone fight one.

"Rorik Glowlimn," intoned the elder, "do you accept your task?"

The word *no* started to form almost automatically on Rorik's lips, but something, perhaps a glance from Urik or the feelingless look on the elder's wrinkled face, made him change his mind. If he was ever going to be anything in life, he must make the right decision now.

"Yes," he said softly, "I do."

Rorik awoke early in the morning of his departure, the memory of the day before still fresh in his mind. He got out of bed and began to dress in clothing similar to Urik's. The only difference was that Rorik's clothes were much newer and did not show traces of previous quests. Rorik's door soon opened and, without a word, Urik Ironarm entered and sat down on Rorik's newly-straightened bed. There was nothing different about the warrior's appearance, except that on his back was a small sack containing things for the trip to Eagle Peak, some eighty kilometers away. Urik strode over to the small table on which Rorik's slightly larger pack was lying. He opened it and began to sort

through its contents. Rorik was shocked to see that
when the warrior finished sorting through everything
Rorik had been sure he would need, there was a large
pile of things which the older man deemed unneces-
sary lying on the wooden floor, and the sack was now
half empty.

"Come on, hurry up!" grunted Urik impatiently.
"Let's start this day early or we'll never get there."
Rorik finished dressing and hurried to the door.

"You're not forgetting anything, are you?" asked
Urik. In his hand was Rorik's bag, which the boy had
overlooked. Embarrassed, Rorik took the bag from
him and led the way out of the wooden house and
into the village square. As they were walking through
the village, Rorik thought he caught glimpses of people looking at him from the small windows of their
houses. He walked with his head bent low.

"Is that any way to go out on a quest?" snapped
Urik. "With your head down like that, you look as if
you're on your way to a burial."

I am, thought Rorik. *My own.*

"Well," continued the warrior in his gruff manner,
but this time with a hint of affection in his voice, "if
you really must hide your head, I've brought you something proper to hide it under." It was then that Rorik
noticed that his companion's hands were not empty.
In them was a small mesh bag which he now opened
and, after removing its contents, discarded at the side
of the path. From the bag he produced a helmet much
like the one he himself wore, made of metal and with
two tufts of brightly colored feathers. This he put without a word on Rorik's head and then walked slightly
ahead. Rorik felt like thanking the warrior, but he knew

that Urik was trying to avoid further discussion. So he followed silently.

He followed silently, in fact, for the rest of that uneventful day of hiking, except for the occasional pauses in which Urik pointed out exactly where they were. And all through the day the menacing peak grew closer and closer, and home was further away.

They stopped late that evening under Eagle Peak. Just in time, too, for Rorik was sure he could take no more of the rugged terrain. They cooked a small dinner and went to sleep without a word, tomorrow's climb in both their minds.

When Rorik awoke, it was still dark, with only a hint of early morning sunlight over the hills.

"Why so early?" asked Rorik as he stretched his tired muscles.

"If we don't finish the climb while the sun is still on the other side of the peak, we won't be able to reach the top in the midday heat."

They went about gathering their belongings and silently preparing for the climb. When they were done, Urik handed Rorik a pair of picks, and they began the climb. Although the peak was not extremely high, it was a difficult climb, and were it not for the picks, Rorik would have fallen several times. They reached the summit's plateau just as the noonday sun began to scorch the cliff face they had just climbed.

"You see," said Urik, "try to climb it in this light and see how far you get."

The rest of the day was spent searching out various cave entrances for traces of the sandgorgon. The inside of the peak, Urik explained, was virtually hollow and was a maze of tunnels and caves. By the end of the day, the pair had singled out two entrances in which the sandgorgon might be hiding. The kill, Urik said, would have to be on the next day or the day after, since they had only six days to return to the village with the head of the monster. Rorik was not so eager. He was inclined to procrastinate for as long as possible—which, as it happened, was not so long.

Rorik awakened the next morning to the sounds of vicious hisses, a sword slicing the air, and war cries from Urik Ironarm. It was then that he got his first look at a sandgorgon. The creature was like an immense iguana, with a spiked tail and teeth easily a quarter of a meter long. Its sharp, hooked foreclaws were making brutal slashes at Urik, who was doing his best to ward the beast off. The stakes were evident: if Urik was not successful, he would be driven off the edge of the cliff.

Rorik grabbed his sword, slapped on his helmet, said a quick prayer to one deity or another, and yelled, "Hang on, Urik, I'm coming!"

Almost instantly, though he knew not why, Rorik saw what had to be done. Giving a loud yell to distract the sandgorgon's attention, he raised his sword above his head and, with all his strength, brought the sharp edge of the blade down on the creature's tail. The gash it made was a small one, but enough to make the creature turn to face its new opponent. As it was turning, it made one final slash at Urik's chest and, as the claw withdrew, Rorik thought he saw something in the claw catch the morning sunlight. While the side of the creature was facing Urik, he used this opportunity to stab the underpart of the sandgorgon. In the agony of this stab, the creature leaped straight at Rorik.

This is the end, thought Rorik, as the sandgorgon's huge body bore down on him. Then he saw his chance. As the monster's huge body passed over him, Rorik, sword held high, ran under it, slashing the beast's soft belly. The sandgorgon hit the ground with a tremendous thump and scurried down the nearest cave entrance as fast as its damaged body would allow.

Now that the danger had passed, Rorik suddenly felt the shock of what he had done. The thought of it made him sit down on a rock to gather his senses before he collapsed in exhaustion. It was then that he noticed Urik. He too was sitting on a rock, but on his face was a look Rorik had never seen before. He was staring at his chest. As soon as Rorik looked, he too saw the thing that had caused the warrior's look of horror.

Urik's life-giving gem was gone!

The implications of this took a while to sink into Rorik's mind. Without the gem, Urik had said that he could live perhaps a day more. Slowly, Rorik got up and walked over to Urik.

"What do we do now?" he asked quietly.

"That is up to you," said Urik. "If you wish me to live, it is for you to go into the cave and kill the sandgorgon. This would not be easy, for he is enraged. Your actions just now were commendable; they proved, as I had hoped, that you work well under pressure. I do not know whether it was the sword or you who controlled your actions. I think, however, that you are capable of killing the sandgorgon."

This was the longest speech Rorik had ever heard

Urik make, and it raised a question in his mind. Had Urik purposely lured the beast out, knowing that Rorik would be forced to act?

There was, however, no time to think about this. Rorik picked up his sword and, without a glance back at Urik, entered the cave. He knew its layout; they had explored it the day before. He took a torch from his pack, lit it, and started down the dark passageway.

He had barely entered the room when he noticed the creature. It was lying against the far wall with its head facing Rorik. Slowly, the sandgorgon opened its mouth and, as if blowing out a match, blew a gust of air across the room, dousing Rorik's torch.

Rorik did not have time to light another one before the sandgorgon was upon him. He caught a glimpse of the gem lodged in the creature's claw as it came straight down at his head.

Suddenly, just as before, Rorik knew what to do. A strange feeling came over him, sort of like a shiver, starting at his head and running down through his arm to the sword. Then the sword began to glow. Slowly it lit up until Rorik could see his surroundings clearly. He saw the sandgorgon and felt a strange emotion. It was hate and wildness—there was no fear and no pity for the beast.

Rorik, almost in a trance, raised the sword and brought it straight down onto the creature's forehead. A howl went up from the sandgorgon's throat, a howl of agony and defeat. Back on the plateau, Urik Ironarm heard the howl and smiled . . .

The story of the gem goes on to reveal that Urik

Ironarm and Rorik Glowlimn returned safely to their village where they each went on to live, as we hear in fairy tales, "happily ever after." Rorik followed the family tradition and became an armorer. It is even said that he fashioned a sword more powerful than his own. In any case, he never went fighting again. Urik Ironarm lived for twenty more years until one night when he was killed in a blaze that also destroyed his home. The gem in which this story is written was Urik's life-giving gem. I will always wear the gem in hopes that it may extend my life, but I think the magic has long gone out of it. The gem probably relied on Urik's strong will to live as much as Urik relied on the gem.

ABOUT THE AUTHOR

Jonah Steinberg, a Canadian, attends the American International School in Vienna, Austria. Mr. Steinberg enjoys theater production and specializes in lighting design. He wrote this story while in the eighth grade.

A Speck in Infinity

by JULIE WILSON

My name is Joanne Lowe," she wrote, then paused. "*Tomorrow I am going to orbit the Earth,*" she added. She reread what she had written, and it seemed clumsy and untalented. What a time to come down with a case of writer's block! The entire world was depending on her to make outer space real to them. Why did they all think that she, Joanne Lowe, could perform the impossible? Frustrated, she abandoned her writing and tried to relax.

My umbilical cord to Earth has been stretched almost beyond repair. I miss Earth. She is a mother, beside whom I feel like the smallest child. Once I lay on her surface and felt her heartbeat, steady and deep. She loomed gigantic underneath me, and I loved her secure size. I clung to her. I thought: Later, when my body rots, I shall be a part of her. Not dust to dust: child to mother.

Feeling unimportant, Joanne was hustled through

the corridors of NASA for a last-minute conference with Captain Fogg. She was escorted into an antiseptic, gray-walled lounge, and she sat in a plastic chair.

Captain Fogg was a hearty man with a red, bovine face and a sturdy physique. Joanne had a distrust for this kind of man. You never knew what he was thinking behind his mask of over-friendliness. He treated her a little too jovially, so she suspected that he secretly disliked her.

"Well, Joanne," he said, "ready for liftoff?"

Joanne tried to smile. "Sure."

"Good, good." He leaned back, seeming to survey her.

"Joanne," he said finally. The ubiquitous smile was still lurking on his face. "Do you realize that you're not really equipped for a space voyage? You have no scientific background. From the first, I opposed allowing a layman onto Stargazer III." He halted, watching her. "You're just . . . extra trouble for the crew."

Joanne knew that her ears were turning red. She hated this tendency of hers to blush in any tense situation. She responded hotly to the captain's words.

"Sir, I am not exactly a layman. I am very well qualified for my job, which is to write my impressions of outer space. You recall, in 1998 I won the Pulitzer—"

"Yes, yes. But you know pitifully little of value to the crew. Our ship is designed for economy: we have as few people on it as possible. You are essentially one hundred twenty pounds of empty space."

Joanne pursed her lips. "I—"

"Anyway, Joanne, I want you to know your place. You are to keep completely out of the way of the crew, and at no time disobey orders. Is that clear?"

"I have been fully briefed by NASA," Joanne said stiffly. "I won't be in the way."

"Good."

Stars. They are both little and big at the same time. To me, they look as small as the freckle on my wrist, but I am told that most are many times the size of Earth. I see them in the light of my own mortality. Stars are incredibly hot: gargantuan deathtraps. When I envision a star, I mentally throw myself into that giant inferno. On clear nights I go outside and recite the child's rhyme: "Star light, star bright . . ." Then I make a wish. But the only thing that star could give me is death.

The countdown started. As Joanne sat tensely strapped to her chair, she waited for the fateful number zero.

The woman beside her, Katie Barclow, smiled at Joanne's look of terror. "Nervous?" she asked, but it was a rhetorical question. "Takeoff's nothing to worry about. I've done this hundreds of times, and it's never affected me in the slightest."

"I guess I *am* nervous. It's my first time."

"Uh-huh. Excited?"

"Yeah, I guess. But mostly I'm terrified."

"Oh, everyone's scared on their first trip."

Joanne realized that it was not so much the danger of the trip that she was afraid of. It was the responsibility that really preyed on her mind. All of Earth was hanging on her every word as it was radioed to them. What if she couldn't think of anything to say?

Oh, to be elevated above the rest of the human race! To be above is to be superior. I can understand Icarus's desire to fly to the sun. I have always dreamed of flying. I would imagine that I was sitting on a cloud, look-

*ing down on the land below. An anthill! Wide high-
ways would be threads of silver. Cars would be multi-
colored beetles, scurrying with a false sense of urgency.
I tried to fly like a bird, but failed. I was not destined
to become a giant.*

Joanne spent most of those first few days looking
out into the blackness of space. It was monotonous,
yet it exerted a kind of hypnotic influence over her.
She had not yet written anything.

It was plain that Joanne was not needed on the
spaceship. The crew was forever busy, hurrying places,
adjusting machines, and speaking in unintelligible tech-
nical jargon. She was sure they resented her idleness.
Captain Fogg was barely polite. Some of them—Katie,
for instance—seemed to like her. Still, she felt like a
stowaway on the Stargazer III.

*The atoms that make up my body consist of pro-
tons, neutrons, and electrons. Between these particles
an infinite amount of space exists. In this way the human body is similar to the galaxy.*

*I am ninety-nine percent space. But if I am space,
how can I be the human being who loves and hates?
Particles cannot feel emotions. An electron is an electron is an electron. My electrons look just like anyone
else's. There is a danger in thinking too small: you lose
your sense of self.*

Joanne stared at her computer terminal. Its blank
face was accusing. It screamed aloud her insufficiency.

Yesterday, Captain Fogg had called her to his conference room. He had asked her what she had written, and she had had to admit that she had written
nothing as of yet. He seemed about to say something
and then stopped. She knew what he had been think-

ing: "One hundred twenty pounds of empty space."

She got up and went to peer at the stars. "How can I describe them?" she thought desperately. As she looked, she suddenly felt a familiar surge of power wash over her: inspiration.

She sprang for her computer terminal. She wrote: "I am a speck in infinity."

To journey into space is to realize fully your own unimportance. The evidence of eons is gathered here. What lasting stamp can I, a speck in infinity, place on the universe? I will be dead in decades, but space will live forever. All evidence of my presence will be dust in a thousand years, but space will last forever. Earth itself will perish in a few million years, but space will always exist. If I had to choose one word to describe space, it would be "time."

About the Author

Julie Wilson lives in Arlington, Virginia, and attends Yorktown High School. Her interests include swimming, writing, travel, and languages. She wrote this story while in the tenth grade.

Local Heroes

The Cormorant in My Bathtub

by BROOKE ROGERS

When I was about eight, I went to live with my grandparents at the beach. I had never seen the ocean before, and to this day the memory is vivid. We pulled into the driveway at dusk, and I could see behind the house an exciting expanse of untouched water. I shivered. Since my parents' death, I had not felt any emotion; I had been only a breathing vegetable. But now I could feel the blood beginning to pump through my veins. I felt warm and tingly. The colors of the horizon and the dying sun were a shimmer of pinks and purples. The sun, arrayed in its most beautiful gown, was ready to die valiantly. I was sure even the Garden of Eden could not have been more beautiful.

From that moment on I was madly in love with the ocean. I lay in the sand for hours watching the cormorants circling over the lapping waves. How I envied those birds, their graceful black bodies circling and diving into the brilliant waters. They did not know fear or sadness; they knew only life, sun, and the ocean. They would plummet into the sea at tremendous speeds, and not once did they miss their prey. There were no failures. Each one always emerged with a silver minnow speared on its beak.

Every day from sunup to sundown I haunted the beach. I never tried to make new friends; I was always alone. I dreaded the first day of school. I was always dreaming that I would become a cormorant and fly away over the ocean, never to be seen again.

It was a Wednesday night when the tanker sank. The rain was falling in solid sheets, the wind blowing at nearly fifty knots! All the power lines were out; even the glow of the lighthouse was not strong enough to pierce the storm. The captain of the tanker lost his course and ran aground on Lookout Point. The side of the tanker split on the rocks, spilling hundreds of thousands of gallons of oil into the raging sea.

The next day the ocean was calm, but the waves that lapped against the beach were tainted. Riding on the waves were the black remains of the oil tanker's cargo. I watched in horror as helpless sea birds struggled to stay afloat, flapping their wings in frenzied splashes as they tried desperately to free themselves from the clinging oil. Tears streamed down my cheeks as I dashed into the ocean and gathered up as many birds as I could capture. I returned to the house and filled the bathtub with clean, fresh water. Then I pried open as many beaks as I could. I watched helplessly as the birds surrendered to the clinging grease that clogged their nostrils and held fast their beaks. My whole body shook with grief. I lifted their limp bodies and tenderly set them on a towel. Among the dead were three gulls, two sandpipers, and one brown pelican.

One bird remained in the tub, a black bird who would not give up. He lay quietly in the tub, but his eyes were alert, and he was wide awake. He was a cormorant. To take my mind off the others, I picked him up and began to rub his back with tissue and detergent. It took hours, but the bird seemed to sense that I was trying to help. He lay still and allowed me to wipe every last drop of oil off his glossy back. When I placed him back in the tub he drank deeply, enjoying the strange, sweet taste of fresh water for the first time.

When my grandma found me she did not scold me for making a mess of her guest bathroom. She simply asked if I would like some help burying the dead birds. Without asking, I knew she would let the cormorant stay in her bathtub. The bird was clearly exhausted. He lay motionless with his head tucked under his wing. As we buried the six birds, I wondered what would happen to the seventh.

For a week my grandparents forbade me to visit the beach. I knew that the oil was still thick and that the white sand would never be quite as pure. We had numerous wildlife representatives visit our beach and collect water samples and gather up dead fish and birds. They would often stop and look in on my bird, but they never tried to take him away. I fed him sardines and tuna fish. He ate greedily and slowly became stronger. Sadly, I realized that my new friend would need to leave me.

A few kids in my neighborhood stopped by to see

the bird. Grandma encouraged them to stay for tea, and I was surprised at how much fun we had. The more time I spent with the neighborhood kids, the more I looked forward to the opening of school. The water was regaining its purity and soon it would be safe to let my bird go. He would once again be searching the sea for a school of minnows instead of splashing about in our bathtub. Still, I did not like to think about losing him.

Two weeks after the storm, school started. I was excited by new classes and new friends. I was spending very little time on the beach. Instead, I had been playing baseball in the lot behind our house. I felt needed and wanted for the first time since my parents' death; the black bird in my bathtub needed me, and my friends wanted me to play third base and share adventures with them.

On the third day of school I returned home to find the bird gone. The door was shut tight, but the window was open and the curtain was blowing in the breeze. On the floor below the window a long black feather rested. I picked it up and stroked the smooth edge as I thought of all the bird had given me.

ABOUT THE AUTHOR

Brooke Rogers lives in Olympia, Washington, and attends Charles Wright Academy in Tacoma. She has a collection of pets, including two dogs, two ducks, one hamster, one rabbit, and three cats. Her other interests are tennis, swimming, and sailing. She wrote this story while in the seventh grade.

Like One of the Family

by KATHLEEN LATZONI

He followed me all the way home, Mom." Joey Kinley shifted from one foot to the other as if he had springs attached to his feet. "Can I keep him?"

Mrs. Kinley stopped to consider. The "him" in question was a pale, thin young man in his late teens, with a black beret resting on his neck-length blond hair—obviously an Irregular, she thought, from the uneven glint in his eyes.

"Maybe," she said. "What's his name?"

"Gee, I don't know. He didn't talk to me the whole time."

"All right." She turned to the Irregular. "Do you know what your name is?" she asked, speaking softly.

He looked up for the first time, an inane half-moon grin on his face. "Yes—but I don't have to tell you." The last word dissolved into a shrill giggle.

"Oh, come on." Patience would take her only so

far, but she'd try at least one more time. "You want to tell me, don't you?"

"OK . . . it's Andy. Happy?" He didn't wait for an answer before starting to giggle again.

"Yes—very. Now . . . Andy, why don't you and Joey—you did tell him your name, didn't you, Joey?—go find something to do outside. I'll be busy." She guided them toward the door. "If he's going to stay, I have to get things ready for him."

"I can keep him? Great! Thanks, Mom." Joey rushed outside, taking Andy with him.

Mrs. Kinley watched them until they disappeared around the corner. Well, she should have expected it. Ever since Marcia down at the office had gotten her daughter an Irregular . . . She closed the door, thinking about the way Joey had acted, banging around the house as if he were looking for something but didn't know what.

But Marcia's Irregular never did any more than see things stirring in the night—she wasn't so sure about Andy. Suppose, God forbid, he attacked her or Joey . . . He'll need a place to sleep, she reflected, as she turned her thoughts back to the practical. Maybe the den; he could use Joey's old sleeping bag. She headed upstairs to get it, remembering New Year's Eve, 1999—how many years ago was it now? Joey had been just a baby when the president had made his announcement.

She and her husband, Mike, had been watching the New Year's Eve broadcast from Times Square when the screen went blank, and then there was a message reading SPECIAL NEWS FLASH.

"What the . . ." Mike sat up and put his drink down.

"I don't know," she said. "I hope it doesn't run through midnight—"

"Good evening," a well-dressed reporter said. "Today the White House announced a landmark decision. In an attempt to keep up with the growing national debt, it announced that all government-operated mental institutions will soon be closed. We spoke with the president . . ."

"Did you hear that?" she asked. "They're closing the institutions. That means they're going to let crazy people out, Mike—they'll be wandering around all over the place. Suppose one of them gets hold of a gun or something . . ." She had named her biggest fear, and it was all she could say while the reporter kept on talking on the screen.

Now the cameras were inside the White House, where the president was seated in a chair, looking ready to answer any and all questions. "I realize a lot of people may see this as a drastic move," he said, "but it's one of many steps we'll have to take if we intend to balance the budget. After all, there are many other federal programs that are absolute necessities—"

But you could cut back on them anyway, Mrs. Kinley thought. There must be something else . . . anything . . . just don't let those crazy people out!

The president couldn't hear her. "As the institutions close, we'll gradually start releasing people and classifying them as Irregulars, doing as much as we can to establish separate communities for them—and then we'll encourage the state- and privately-owned institutions to do the same thing." He smiled. "We hope to have the program fully in place by 2003."

That had been all, except for the anchorman's fi-

nal comments before the network returned to the New
Year's Eve program. And I've hardly had to worry at
all, Mrs. Kinley thought as she got the sleeping bag
down from the shelf. For the most part, the Irregulars
stayed in their own communities, like her own town's
East End.

Mrs. Kinley carted the bag into the den. Maybe
things hadn't worked out quite as the White House
had planned, but then 2000 had been a year for hasty
promises—like she and Mike saying they'd stay mar-
ried forever. "Forever" had lasted nine years, she thought
bitterly, rolling the sleeping bag out with a sudden jerk.
She stared at it, dusty and wrinkled with disuse, and
thought about the president and Joey and Andy outside, and suddenly she didn't know whether the whole
thing was supposed to be funny or sad.

The air was still gray with chill when Mrs. Kinley
got up the next morning. Things had gone better than
she'd thought—no calls from Joey, no frantic, sense-
less cries in the middle of the night. She sleepily came
downstairs and stopped at the doorway of the den.
No sound but the soft noise of breathing. She continued into the kitchen.

She got the coffee out and began to search for the
cereal, as if today's breakfast would be like others.
Maybe Marcia would have some idea of what to feed
the Irregular.

"Good morning."

Andy stood in the doorway for a second before
coming in. "I didn't know you were awake yet," he
said.

"I didn't know *you* were." She watched his move-
ments carefully, laughing nervously as she closed the

cupboard door. "How did you sleep? I can get you a blanket if you—"

"No, I was just fine." He sat down at the kitchen table; she did not. "I guess I make you pretty nervous, huh?"

"What? Oh—oh, no. You don't. It's just that I'm used to being alone first thing in the morning, and—well, you startled me, that's all. I thought you were asleep . . ."

He smiled ruefully, as if he knew she was lying. Suddenly she realized what was making her nervous: he seemed different today. Perfectly normal.

"You can stop with the excuses," he said. "I can understand how you feel. So you don't have to . . . don't . . . have . . . to . . ." He lapsed into silence for a few minutes. Then, although nothing had happened, Andy burst out with a series of loud, almost screeching laughs that were all the worse because there was no humor behind them.

Mrs. Kinley stood and watched, frozen in place. The noise was horrible, almost more than she could stand, and she wanted to yell back at Andy, or hit him, anything so he'd stop. But she couldn't, because even when the laughter turned into a high-speed, half-mumbled chatter of words, she kept remembering that only a minute ago they had actually talked—as if he had been another person.

"Some of them do that quite often." Marcia plunked a stack of papers on Mrs. Kinley's desk, then sat down. "They don't know what causes it, but I've heard of Irregulars like that—they could be talking to you one minute and just go out of control the next." She paused, frowning. "Of course, it could have something to do with how you treat them. You've never been very good at discipline, Susan—"

"I know. You've told me that before." Mrs. Kinley tapped a pencil impatiently against the arm of her chair. She didn't particularly like Marcia, but she had to admit that the young woman had a lot of information. And it was almost always right. "So, what are you supposed to do with them?"

"Well, the important thing to remember is, you've got to always treat them the same, no matter how they act. Otherwise, they'll get confused and be worse than before. And you've got to stay in control." She finished, leaned back, and then, as if she had just remembered something, handed Mrs. Kinley a piece of paper. "I was supposed to give you this," she said. "The secretary wanted you to see it."

Mrs. Kinley glanced at the paper. It was a standard patient-release form, just like the ones that Susan Kinley, Assistant Hospital Director, had to sign every day. But this one was headed: SPECIAL NOTICE—FORWARD TO ASSISTANT DIRECTOR IMMEDIATELY.

"An Irregular, hmm?" Mrs. Kinley said after reading the first few lines. "Sixteen-year-old Caucasian female. Is she the one who was in that accident?"

"That's her," Marcia sighed. "Some guy was driving along when she just stepped out into the middle of the road and sat down. Of course, he couldn't stop in time. And that's why we've got her on our hands."

"So?" She wondered what Marcia was getting at. "Is there some kind of problem with her, or—"

"No, she's fine now. After five hours in surgery,

that is. But the man who hit her won't pay the bill. And of course *she* can't pay it. But if we let one Irregular go without paying, we'll have to do that for all of them. Can you imagine," she asked, leaning forward again, "what that would do to the budget?"

"Oh, come on, Marcia. So the hospital absorbs a few costs. It's built into the budget anyway."

"Not any more. Not since we stopped getting federal aid. We're the closest hospital to the East End. If this gets out, they'll come pouring in—you know how many accidents they have over there."

"No, actually, I don't." Mrs. Kinley wished Marcia would get to the point; this whole conversation was making her uncomfortable.

"Well, I suggest you go down there sometime and see for yourself. Anyway, here's what that note is about. We've got her heavily sedated up on the sixth floor. It would be easy for some doctor to just put a needle in her arm . . . give her more sedative than she really needs. And it would be purely an accident, if anyone asks. Which they probably won't."

"You mean they're going to kill her?" Mrs. Kinley hardly heard her own voice come out.

"Why not? It's about our only choice—I just told you what would happen if we let her go. Besides, it's not as if she were someone *normal*. After all, Susan, what kind of life is *that* to preserve?"

"Yes . . . yes, I suppose so, but . . ." She studied the wall behind Marcia, but it couldn't tell her what to do or what to think, not even if she begged it to.

"There aren't any buts. Believe me, they can't really feel. They just exist, that's all." She paused, then smiled. "Of course, I'm not the assistant director. It's up to you to choose. You've got till Friday." Marcia got up to leave, glancing at the clock. "Well, see you at lunch."

Mrs. Kinley didn't look up as Marcia went out the door. She stared blankly at the paper in her hands. The words on it had seemed so clear just a minute before . . . Well, you wanted this promotion, she told herself. If you want to keep this position, you'll have to make decisions.

"That's true," she said out loud, suddenly seeing Andy's face in the back of her mind. "But not until Friday."

When Mrs. Kinley pulled into her driveway that afternoon, she remembered: Andy had been alone all day, until Joey came home, and then Joey had been in the house alone with him.

"Joey!" she called as she strode quickly into the house. "How are you?" She paused, then added, "How's Andy?"

"Fine, Mom. We're both fine." Joey appeared from the kitchen.

"Good. Nothing—you know, happened?"

"No. Andy was in the den. I couldn't get him to play with me or anything. Anyway, how come you asked?" he demanded suddenly. "I'm old enough to take care of him. You never think I can do any—"

"Yes, yes, I know, and it was very good of you to look after him," she said hastily by way of consolation as she rushed into the den. If he'd hurt himself, or broken anything . . .

Andy was sitting in a corner, legs bent and drawn up close to his body. He was mumbling to himself, things that sounded like quotes from some strange book only he had read.

"Andy," she said, touching his shoulder.

He looked up, again with a vacant smile. "Oh . . . hi. I'm talking to my friends. Want to come?"

"No, that's all right. Did anything happen to you today?" Too late, it occurred to her that he probably wouldn't remember.

"Nothing to me—but to my friends . . ." He went on as she left. Well, Mrs. Kinley thought, if all he was going to do was sit in a corner and talk to his "friends," then maybe it hadn't been such a bad idea after all.

The next day, the situation at the office was enough to make anyone a nervous wreck. Marcia had been getting the whole place worked up about the Irregular, and each of Mrs. Kinley's employees kept coming in, one at a time, to tell her what they would do, if *they* had to make the decision.

"Well, thank you. That's a good idea, and I'll have to consider it," Mrs. Kinley said once again, this time to somebody-or-other's secretary. "But it's five o'clock—" Thank God, she thought, glancing at her watch—"and I'd like to get home. If you don't mind . . ."

"Oh, no, sure." The woman got up and left. Mrs. Kinley watched her go, smiling with relief. She kept smiling all the way home, thinking that she could sit down awhile before making supper, watch some TV, relax.

The house was empty when she walked in. Joey had said he'd be late today, she remembered, but Andy . . . She went from room to room, her pace growing faster as he failed to turn up. Not in the living room, not in the kitchen, not in the den . . . I'm not worried. Why should I be worried? He's got to be here. I'm perfectly calm, she told herself, even when Andy wasn't upstairs either.

She stepped outside onto the sidewalk and took a quick glance up and down the street, but there was no one around. Up the street first, she decided. I'm not worried, I'm not worried, I'm not worried . . .

Andy was standing on the street corner, watching the cars go by as if he'd never seen such movement before in his life. *Just stepped out into the middle of the street . . . the driver couldn't stop in time . . .*

Mrs. Kinley raced up to him, grabbing his hand roughly. "Come with me," she said, the words coming out as hard and tight as the knot in her stomach. She pulled Andy back inside the house without a word and set him in the middle of the living room.

"Why did you do that?" She didn't expect an answer or even want one. "You're supposed to stay here—don't you even know that much? Don't you know *anything*?"

He wasn't listening, she knew that; he was just hearing the sounds of the words. "Don't you know anything," he repeated dully. "Don't you don't you know anything anything anything—" The words got faster and faster, the syllables all slurring into one another.

"Shut up!" she screamed, feeling suddenly helpless and out of control. She had to make him listen to her. "Stop it," she said, a little calmer. He kept on, not paying any attention. "Just STOP IT!"

"Stop it." Now he was even using her voice, as close to it as he could come. "Stop it stop it stop it stop it—"

She hit him.

It was exactly what he didn't need. Before Mrs. Kinley could do anything, Andy had pulled away from her with a crazy scream. He wheeled around the living room, smashing things, throwing things, knocking things over.

Mrs. Kinley got hold of him, grabbing his arms so he couldn't hit back. He turned around, and she saw his eyes. One look told her how lost and scared he must feel, and she felt ashamed for what she'd done.

"I'm sorry," she whispered, as soon as he had calmed down. "I couldn't help it. It's been a long day, and then you were gone, and I was worried about you, and . . . I just couldn't help it. That's all."

Andy looked straight at her. His mouth was working furiously, as if he was trying to say something. Finally, it came out. "Home," he said. "*Home.*"

"Home? Yes, you're home now. This is where you live." Mrs. Kinley wondered what he was talking about.

He shook his head. "No. *Home,*" he repeated, this time pointing to the door. "Eeaaass . . . End. Go home." Andy pointed to himself, then at the door again.

Suddenly it dawned on her. "Oh . . . that's why you left the house. You were trying to get home, weren't you? To the East End." She laid a comforting hand on his shoulder. "Well, don't worry. I'll drive you there—but only for a short visit. Just wait until I get home tomorrow."

Mrs. Kinley edged the car along the side of the street, wondering if this was the right way to the East End—she never could remember directions. Inwardly she sighed with relief when she saw the big sign, al-

most the size of a billboard, ahead of her on the road.
WARNING: RESTRICTED AREA. LIMITED ADMIT-
TANCE BETWEEN 8 A.M. AND 6 P.M. NO ADMIT-
TANCE BETWEEN 6 P.M. AND 8 A.M.

"That means we'll have to hurry," Mrs. Kinley said,
turning to Andy in the back seat of the car. "We've
only got a half-hour . . ." Her words trailed off when
she realized that Andy wasn't listening to her. Instead,
he had his face pressed against the car window, peering out intently.

Someone darted out in front of her car, and she
quickly slammed on the brakes. Marcia had said there
were a lot of accidents around here. No wonder. "Well,
this is it," she said, this time keeping her eyes on the
road. "We're in the East End."

"I know," Andy mumbled. He kept looking out the
window as Mrs. Kinley drove on.

Even though she was trying to be a careful driver,
she couldn't help paying more attention to the people
than to the streets. Men and women, all races, crowded
every sidewalk, leaving no space to walk or even move.
They were wearing either clothes that were worn almost to rags or cheap, poorly sewn garments. Most of
them were staring into space or wandering around aim-
lessly, talking to themselves. Some were leaning out
of the windows of broken-down apartment buildings
that seemed to go up forever. A few were crying. And
one boy and one girl were . . . My God, Mrs. Kinley
thought, right in the street! She turned her head away,
but couldn't shut out what was all around her. The
noise, the confusion, the filth that was everywhere was
overwhelming. Why hadn't she known? Why didn't
they show it on television? Doesn't anyone know, she

felt like screaming, how they live?

She wanted to get out as fast as possible, but they had to stop the car again, this time for an expensive sedan in front of them. It pulled over to the curb. A young woman, dressed in a beautiful, tailored suit, got out. She stood still, looking around with confusion and fear in her eyes. Some people don't have any sense, Mrs. Kinley thought irritably. Imagine showing all this to a young thing like her. It was obvious that she couldn't handle it. Well, at least if she didn't appreciate her own life before this, she would now.

The sedan door closed. While Mrs. Kinley watched, whoever was in it drove quickly away, leaving the girl behind on the sidewalk. The girl's eyes and mouth widened into a trio of circles. "Mama," she said, the way a baby would, but the sedan, of course, didn't slow down. "Mommy! Mama . . . Ma—MAAAAAA!" As she kept on screaming, her hands flew up to her chest. Long pink fingernails tore at the delicate wool jacket, then at the skirt. Finally, when her clothes were as much in rags as everyone else's, she sank to the ground and curled up in a ball. No one who passed her on the street noticed her—or, if they did, paid any attention.

Mrs. Kinley watched, numb. For a minute, she thought of chasing the sedan and getting them to come back. But that was impossible. She had no idea which way the sedan went, and even if they did catch them, what could she say? Take back your daughter and be a criminal?

"My parents left me like that," Andy said suddenly. Mrs. Kinley stared at him; she never would get used to the way his thoughts changed to normal so suddenly. "But I was younger than her, of course."

"Does . . . every family do that?" she asked. She couldn't get the image of the girl out of her mind. "Just drop them off on the sidewalk and not look back?"

"Eventually. There's no particular age limit—it's just whenever the parent admits that they don't have a 'normal' child." He smiled wryly. "Her parents must have had more patience than mine."

"I'm sorry. I didn't know . . ." They weren't the right words, she was sure. The right words were somewhere inside her, but somehow when she looked at Andy's face, she couldn't get them to come forth.

"Please. Don't bother about it." He paused, looked at the girl again for a second, then turned back to her. "You didn't realize at first, did you? You saw her on the sidewalk and thought she was just visiting. Imagine," he leaned back against the car seat. "She's got one in her own house—and she still can't tell the difference."

Mrs. Kinley didn't answer. When Andy's thoughts were clear, he was very perceptive—too much so, she thought. He was right—she *hadn't* been able to tell that the girl was an Irregular. She kept on driving, past the sign that read YOU ARE NOW LEAVING A RE-STRICTED AREA. There was a thought growing in her head, one so strange and new that she wanted, at first, to push it away, but it kept on insistently: *If you couldn't tell the difference—and you've seen so many of them—then maybe the difference isn't so big after all.*

Mrs. Kinley watched the Irregular lying in her hospital bed. The age on the release form read sixteen, but she looked much younger, with brown hair that hung in a tangled mass around her shoulders and the dull, unfocused look of drugged sleep.

"See what I mean?" Marcia said as she came up behind Mrs. Kinley. "It's obvious what's wrong just from looking at her. Still," she added, putting her hand cheerfully on Mrs. Kinley's shoulder, "you never know. She might have been a nice girl. It's a pity—"

"Marcia." Mrs. Kinley stopped her. "I was going to tell you—I'm signing the release papers. She'll be taken off the sedative tomorrow." The words came out thin and hesitant, hardly the confident tone she'd practiced. She saw the look on Marcia's face; obviously Marcia didn't understand. "I just don't think it's right, that's all—"

"It's not *right*?" Marcia interrupted. "Susan, what's happened? You're usually so practical. This is the hospital's money, remember?"

"Yes, I remember," Mrs. Kinley said slowly. "I remember something else, too. Remember when you told me to go down to the East End and see what it was like? Do you remember that, Marcia?"

"Yes, yes, I do. But what does this have to do with anything?" she asked impatiently.

"It has a lot to do with a lot of things." She started talking faster and louder, not caring who heard her. "I went down there, Marcia. I saw what it's like. Conditions that, believe me, you would not want to spend one *day* in, let alone your *life*—"

"But it's *not* me. It's *them*. Do you really think that they care?"

"Maybe some of them don't. Maybe they're past caring. But what I'm trying to say is that it *could* have been you, or any other person in your family. Do you think all those people acted like Irregulars when they were children? Not all of them. Try to imagine what it would be like to grow up perfectly normal, with a family and friends who loved you, and then when you felt yourself going out of control, they drove you far away and left you there—because it was against the law not to." The flow of words stopped for a minute. She paused, took a breath, then faced Marcia again. "Well? Go on. I'm waiting."

"You're being childish, Susan." Marcia sounded tired. "OK, maybe I wouldn't feel good about it, but—"

"That's an understatement. You'd feel betrayed. *Just like they do*—and I *know*. So, in other words, they're responding like you would. Not like animals. Like *humans*. And when you respond like a human, you have as much right to live as any human does. No matter what some people think."

"In other words, you'd like to send her back to that same mess you just described—is that it?" Marcia asked, louder than she had to. "See how illogical it all is? I know you mean well, Susan, but if you'd only *listen*—"

"No, you listen. I know what it's like there better than you do. But rather *that* than being killed because of something you can't control." Mrs. Kinley faced Marcia squarely.

"*But it's ridiculous!*" Marcia had reached the end of her patience. "She goes back there, she tells all the others what happened—"

"She won't go back there," Mrs. Kinley said. "She'll go with me."

There was complete silence for a second. "Oh no," Marcia finally said. "You've already got one. Two would be too much, Susan; it won't be easy by any means."

"I know it won't be easy. But I can do it. Either that—or you throw her away and throw me away with her." She was surprised to find that she really meant it. "Well?" she challenged. "What do you want, Marcia?"

"You're a very determined woman, Susan," Marcia said. Her voice was quiet. She gave Mrs. Kinley one last puzzled look, then turned away.

Mrs. Kinley watched her go, relief settling slowly over her. She had taken on a lot, but she intended to keep her promise, even if she wasn't quite sure how. Never mind, she thought as she headed back to her office. She'd find a way. For one thing, she'd move Andy into Joey's room—somehow a sleeping bag behind the sofa didn't seem right for him. Or for anybody.

"Do you like your new bed?" Mrs. Kinley asked. Joey had been very understanding, she thought, even when he found out he wouldn't have a spare bed for company anymore.

Andy let himself down cautiously on the bed. "It's very nice," he said finally. "Thank you."

"Better than before, right?"

"Yes, you *could* say that." He smiled. "Why'd you move me? Not to be rude, but—"

"That's what I wanted to talk to you about." She took a deep breath and sat down next to him. "I've already told Joey this. There's a girl at the hospital— an Irregular, like you—and she's coming to live with us. Permanently."

"I see." He took a minute to muse over it. "This

girl—does she look like the one in the East End?"

She couldn't help smiling. "No, she doesn't. But I'm telling you, Andy, you're too smart—you know that?"

"Thanks." He smiled back, a wide, real smile this time.

"Don't thank me. It's true." She got up and headed for the door, turning off the light as she went. Just before she left, she paused and turned to face the room again. "I'll introduce you to her tomorrow. All right, Andy?"

There was silence for a long time, and when Mrs. Kinley finally heard a soft voice in the darkness, she realized that Andy was back in his own world again, talking to his friends. But it was all right, she decided. She could look out for him. And Joey, too—he wasn't turning out too badly. She could look after both of them, and this new girl, too, and love them all as well. As she had never loved "normal" people before.

ABOUT THE AUTHOR

Kathleen Latzoni lives in Short Hills, New Jersey, and attends Millburn Sr. High School in Millburn, New Jersey. A winner of several writing prizes, she also enjoys singing and collecting rock memorabilia. Currently, she is working on a novel. This story was written while Miss Latzoni was in the ninth grade at Millburn Jr. High School.

A Northern Light

by ANDREW HEITZMANN

S he remembered the courtship well. How they danced and dove on the surface of the icy, sun-speckled waters of the North. How they trumpeted and wailed like the insane, all the while their brilliant ebony and alabaster plumage shimmering in the light of day. The loons were then to mate and she to produce five beautifully delicate eggs. Far off, a fisherman observed the small family from his advantageous perch astride a partially submerged tree stump. His unmoving stance betrayed the seriousness of his purpose; his was the bearing of a bullfrog awaiting the visit of a rare insect.

Mother Loon remembered her spouse's death all too well. That day, there was something amiss about the odor in the air. Granted, it was spring, yet still the air around the rude nest hidden in the rushes was all too sweet. Her mate, however, fearless as he was, volunteered to gather food for that morning's meal. He waddled out of the nest, right into the shallow water lapping at its edges, and slid dexterously beneath its surface. She, the Mother Loon, kept watch over her rapidly developing brood of five eggs. Father Loon returned late into day with no meal. Instead he died, quickly but painfully, at the edge of his nest, convulsing and squawking as he lost control of his mind and body. Her mate had fallen victim to the lethal poisons which humans had cast into the once-pristine waters. The lake's swells and ripples carried his corpse away before she could even react. So here she was, peering down at her five brownish-gold eggs, contemplating and scrutinizing the present situation. It was late afternoon, and growing devilishly cold. She was voraciously hungry, as hungry as a starving bear, but she would not move. Her eggs would perish if she left them for even a moment now. Mother Loon would have to dine come early afternoon of the next day, leaving her nest for only a short breath of fresh air. Rethinking, she might not feed at all. It was now nightfall, so she stretched upward, turning around in the nest, and then fell asleep on top of her brood.

A bizarre snapping awoke her in the darkness. Mother Loon prepared herself for a battle to the death.

"Coyote!"

It was a word cackled at her by her mother at a very early age. Yet somehow this didn't seem like the vicious carnivore about to disturb her abode. The steps were not four in a sequence pounding the ground sloppily, but two. Carefully, deliberately, they came nearer.

"Man!"

A piercing light thrust through the tall reeds near the back of her nest. A monster with bony ridges over his eyes, his entire face covered by a grotesque, hairy stubble and his skin flecked with mud, poked his frightening bust through the breach where the dazzling light had shone moments before.

"I'll bite his eyes ouuu—!"

Mother Loon was rendered unconscious by a weak vapor and transported overnight to a new lake, this one untainted by noxious methylmercury.

She woke up well into the morning, the air already warming up. She was sitting on her same nest, over her same eggs. Man hadn't left his "foul odor," the one her mother had warned her about, anywhere on her, or even near her. As before, she was situated by a lake's edge with reeds to her back.

By midday, the water around her nest was as warm as the cloudless sky. The wind ruffling her feathers was nowhere near the cold she at one time had known so well. Mother Loon was about to leave the rude shelter to find food when, suddenly, one of her eggs began to stir with life. Two sunrises had passed, and all she had swallowed was a sip of water. She would have to stay with these eggs indefinitely. She felt a tiny beak strain against her underside. Mother Loon allowed that egg to wobble out from under her. And lo and behold! Soon after, a young loonling sat where the egg had once been, blind and chirping for food. She decided that it would have to be risked. She left the nest and slid under the water right into a school of small fish—perfect! Mother Loon returned with one; the other she'd managed to swallow on the way back. Upon returning to her nest, her new loonling was still alive and well, and all eggs were warm. Over the next ten days, she repeated this procedure for the rest of her young. The first- and second-born were already growing their own soft, rudimentary feathers. Mother Loon commended herself on her success.

Mid-spring came quickly, and with it the farmers' fields that needed irrigation. The water level in her corner of the lake fell five feet almost overnight, and food levels left with it. Mother Loon would be stranded far from the water's edge with five young loons who couldn't walk even as far as a reed's length if she didn't act quickly. So, with her eyesight sharp as needles, she scanned the shoreline on the opposite side of the lake. To her luck, it wasn't draining away.

Currents, she could see, would pose a major problem. If she were to brush up against any of the jagged pilings, submerged or otherwise, she would receive a deep laceration. If a predator were to appear, she'd have to run. Diving under the water to chase it away would only subject her unsupervised offspring to the currents, or leave them to be torn to shreds by the pilings, or swallowed whole by that same predator, or even another. Strategy would have to be employed. Her newly hatched two would ride on her back most of the way, and her remaining three would paddle as best they could, struggling along in her wake. If this small convoy were to become disoriented, the light from a distant cabin would guide them. Mother Loon would head toward this cabin, toward the big, northernmost portion of the lake. She would start out with the young after a premature breakfast on the following morning. The overall travel time should amount to a day or slightly more.

"Quiet down, my youngsters. Tomorrow will judge the worth of your blood in the gene pool of our breed and clan. Close your eyes and go to sleep. Heed not the threatening chill or fear of death. Mark me: fear is the death of thought and the herald of defeat! Laugh as I do at my enemies and challenges: *Ooohoo hoo hoo hoo hoo hawt!*"

And her young replied: "*Ooohaw ooo hoo!*"

"You sound like you are sick or dying. Maybe it's just your sleepiness. We'll try again come sunrise."

Sunrise saw the small family having finished its breakfast and preparing to leave its nest.

"One final try at your laughing before our grueling journey begins. Repeat after me: *ooohoo hoo hoo hoo hoo hawt!*"

"*Eww hoo hee hoo ha!*"

"Now is not the time for a lesson in linguistics, but you will learn. Come now, it is time."

Mother Loon then jumped out of the nest and slid into the cold water of dawn. Next came her first-hatched, he being the boldest, eldest and strongest of the five. Then, her second and third, both at once, making a rather large splash (considering their small sizes). Immediately they were under way, the two youngest between her wings folded on her back, and the other three trailing neatly behind in her calm wake. All too soon, sadly enough, the currents jostled the small group out of their reverie. Mother Loon was pushed toward a jagged piling, the sharpest of a deadly lot of ten. It came closer by the second, taking the shape of a spiny heap of driftwood at first, then revealing rusty teeth of metal. She noticed a weaker current ahead of her; about five kicks of her strong legs would push her past this deadly current and safely behind the heap of debris. Forgetting all of her planning, she swerved into the full strength of the current, her young close behind; they then followed her wake as she executed yet another daring maneuver. Suddenly they were speeding across the current, the force of the water plowing into their right sides and all the while nudging them closer and closer to impending death. Abruptly, their fight was ended. The party had reached the weaker current, had been swept past the piling, and was now in calmer, darker waters. The strong currents had been a trick of the wind and drainage, Mother Loon observed.

Alas, they were now in the eyes of their enemies!

"Pickerel! Muskellunge! Pike!"

More warnings issued to her by her mother. These menacing foes would attack swiftly and silently from below.

"Seagull!"

These birds presented the same danger as waterborne predators, only this fury was unleashed from the sky. Limited only by the gulls' preference for young loonlings over adults, this terror was ever a threat.

Mother Loon noticed an excited flock of such gulls not far to the east. A school of minnows, or other baitfish, must be near. It was early afternoon, their feeding hours. Ironically, the same school of minnows that would occupy the gulls to the east and fill them up, making them sluggish, would also attract the deadly fish.

Coming about as she had predicted, the minnows crossed the lake. Mother Loon's current heading: two-thirds of her way across the lake. The water was chilling, the wind picking up just one last puff of air. The sun was to set soon. Late afternoon bathed the family in a ruddy orange light. Her first instinct was to swim very fast, the swift waters brought on by the wind always carrying her nearer to land. But Mother Loon found this speed a bad move, for even now, as she kicked ever so slowly, the loons in her wake were exhausted.

The hit came, as she expected, toward the rear of her hatchlings. Snapping its jaws and jumping into the air at the same time, the great pickerel prepared to feast. Mother Loon picked up her pace, and her frightened hatchlings followed suit. Her youngest loon, the third and last male of the family of six, attempted to readjust his footing, lost his balance, and rolled off of her, pushed out of beak's reach by the wide wake. He flapped his wings feebly in the water, trying to fly away from the jaws of the pickerel clamping around his waist. He laughed at his foe: "*Ooohoo hoo hoo hoo hoo hawt!*"

An unrivaled tremolo! she thought proudly, as she paddled all the faster, her four young loons speeding along with terror in their eyes. Far back, the water caressed, then enveloped the dying young loon as the pickerel dove under water.

"I'll die bravely, as my father did!"

The young loon tried to resist with legs he no longer had. He caught one last glimpse of his sister's underside from his position under water as she, the last of the group, swam to safety. Then came a warm blackness as the great mouth closed around him. The pickerel had secured his feast in his firm jaws and was now diving to the very bottom of the lake to enjoy it.

Mother Loon saw the similarity between the loon she had just lost and her dead mate. She remembered all that she had gone through to get this far. The sky was now a dark black; the light she had expected to find here had been from a tent—long gone with its campers. Mother Loon was now lurching up to some old, deteriorating shreds of a nest which would serve as temporary lodging for her and her young. She allowed the hatchlings to rest beside her, under her wings. The small family then settled down and fell asleep under the starlit sky, with the softly babbling water of the lake lulling their weary souls into a state of peace.

ABOUT THE AUTHOR

Andrew Heitzmann lives in Woodbridge, Virginia, and attends Osbourn Park High School in Manassas, Virginia. He enjoys track, swimming, reading, fishing, cards, chess, and baseball. He wrote this story while in the eighth grade at Herbert J. Saunders Middle School, also in Manassas.

It Rained for Stevie

by JODI ZISLIS

The sun rested on the horizon, its golden glow shining on Stevie's face. The summer's air was warm and the breeze smelled of rain, as if there was going to be a storm. Her family had been back from David's funeral for four hours. They had changed out of their dressy, dark-colored clothes and silently went on about their business. Stevie still wore her black dress which by now had become wrinkled. She gently rocked on her back porch swing; she'd been sitting there since they had come home. Her cheeks sparkled in the fading sun from freshly cried tears. Big salty droplets fell from her face onto her dress.

The back of Stevie's house faced a huge field whose yellowing grasses swayed in the breeze all the way out to the horizon. The field that Stevie's house overlooked was just off a big steep hill. Stevie loved where she lived because her family had the entire hill and field all to themselves. She lived in an ordinary neighborhood with friends, a school, and a grocery store, but because they were out in the country, everything was spread out a little more. Stevie's neighbors were close enough, however, that she could hear them laughing as they played a game of kickball near her house. She wondered bitterly how anyone could be laughing on this miserable day.

Just as Stevie was changing positions on the swing because her leg had fallen asleep, her mother came out to invite her in to dinner. She was a tall, graceful woman whose step was so light that she had often startled people by suddenly appearing behind them. She approached Stevie, a worried expression on her tired face. She gently placed her slender hand on Stevie's shoulder from behind and said softly, "When your Grandpa Joe died, for a whole year I just wasn't sure I could go on living without my father. Then for another year I still cried sometimes." Stevie knew her mother was trying to comfort her, but she also felt that her efforts were useless. Stevie rolled her teary eyes and looked in another direction. Her mother went on, "I know exactly what you're going through, Stephanie." (It wasn't often that her mom called her by her given name.)

"It's all right to feel sad. I know that David was an important part of your life. And the best thing to do when . . ."

"Mom," Stevie interrupted. It wasn't that Stevie wasn't interested but she wasn't in the mood for talking. She just wanted to be alone. Her mother caught the hint of impatience in her daughter's voice.

"Do come in and have a bite to eat. You haven't eaten in two days. Aren't you hungry?" Stevie just shook her head and wished her mother would go back inside. "But a growing fourteen-year-old girl like you needs her—" Stevie shook her head again, more firmly this time. Her mother got the picture. She hadn't meant to nag. She knew what a sensitive time this would be for her daughter and was not hurt by Stevie's attitude toward her. She remembered well the many hours she herself had spent alone when her father died.

Stevie was relieved to hear the screen door closing behind her mother. She was alone again. She had never really considered herself alone before because she had always counted on David to be there for her when she needed someone. But now she was alone for real. David had left her that way. The pain in her heart was greater than it had ever been since things with David had started to go downhill. Stevie never had to deal with such a serious tragedy before except when her dog died; but that could hardly compare to the loss of the closest friend she had ever had. Nothing had ever hurt this much.

She closed her sad green eyes as another big teardrop rolled down her cheek and tumbled to her dress. She clearly remembered the last things she had done with David. The memories flooded through her mind as if they had just happened.

David was beautiful. His sunlit chestnut hair always fell in his eyes when he ran. He had huge, curious hazel eyes always looking for new things. He was good in almost every sport, but was best at running. David was fast. Stevie, among others, admired him and would trade nearly anything to be as swift as David.

Because he ran frequently, he had developed a solid build. He had always been the adventurous, daring type; this made him fun to be with. His easygoing style and great sense of humor added to his lovableness. Stevie knew that there was no such thing as a perfect person but if someone had to be it, David was definitely the one. He was the best friend she'd ever had, and he had been for a long time, ever since the two of them were three years old.

"Let's go!" one of them would always shout as they flew down the hill to race. They raced each other nearly every day. David almost always won, most of the time by a long shot. Occasionally he would purposely stumble to give Stevie a chance to catch up. Then she would win and although she knew she hadn't won fairly, she still felt good. At first, Stevie felt awkward about running against David, but she soon got over the feeling.

When they were very young, neither of them could understand how there could be a place they could see but not get to. This place was the horizon. Nearly every time they'd race they were determined to have the horizon be their finish line. They would stand behind a stick-drawn line in the dirt, then on the shout of "Go!" they'd run. Stevie always ran hard and fast. She'd give it her all, but it just wasn't enough to get past David's swift stride. They'd run and run, but each time they would get to about the place where they thought the horizon should be, they'd find it still that much ahead of them. The two of them would fall down in the golden field, exhausted.

Then there'd be days for staying indoors, when the sky was gray and the air was cold. Stevie could still see those raindrops, dribbling down the window out-

side. The wind blew hard, and every now and then
the two of them could hear a soft rumbling of thun-
der in the distance. She and David both loved the rain
and the fresh clean scent it always left behind. Stevie
was sprawled on her sofa and David sat in an old over-
stuffed chair with his feet propped up on the arm of
the couch. The weather made them feel lazy and they
decided to spend the afternoon occupying themselves
with doing nothing. So they spent the day wasting time,
watching old movies on the VCR, eating popcorn, watching raindrops race to the bottom of the windowpane,
and wasting more time. They always managed to have
so much fun, no matter what they were doing, as long
as they were together.

The roads had dried from the rain the day before
and a bright, sunny, fresh new day was beginning. Stevie
had arrived at David's house around midafternoon.

"Do you wanna watch the late show tonight?" he
asked her enthusiastically. (David was always enthusi-
astic.)

"That is," he added, "if you can stay up!" Stevie
knew he was joking but just for the heck of it she said,
"I bet I can stay up longer than you!"

"So, is it a bet?" he asked.

"Yup. It's a bet!" Stevie confirmed, and they shook
hands on it and laughed.

That night they took their sleeping bags and met
in the field behind Stevie's house. The plan was that
they were going to stay up all night to prove to each
other who could stay up the longest. And that's exactly what they did. They joked and laughed and talked
all night telling ghost stories, jokes, and remembering
the fun times they had had together. Then they would

laugh some more. The air was warm all night and the field was silent and peaceful. The two of them had the night all to themselves.

As the white sun peeked slightly over the edge of the field, Stevie sat up and rubbed the sleep from her eyes. For an instant she'd forgotten where she was. She looked about her and saw the vast field. To her left was David's back. They had both fallen asleep and now the rising sun had awakened Stevie.

Before waking David, she sat for a few minutes looking around her. Everything sparkled from beads of dew that had magically appeared in the night. The stillness of that morning gave Stevie a special feeling. It's the same feeling you get when you look out your window the morning after the first snowfall, before there are footprints or sled tracks, when none of the icicles has broken and everything glistens with a picture-perfect glow. That's how she felt.

Stevie nudged David with her elbow and he mumbled, "Not yet, Mom. Just a few more minutes." Then he sat up and remembered what he was doing there. "Oh!" he said, embarrassed.

"So who won?" Stevie asked, remembering their contest.

"I dunno," he answered as he tried to smooth down his hair. They sat up side by side and, silhouetted against the bright sky, looked into the sunrise.

Trying to make conversation, David said, "Tell me a secret."

"What secret?" Stevie asked, totally bewildered by his odd request.

"Any secret," he answered.

"OK," she said. "You can't tell anybody though,

OK?" David nodded hastily.

". . . I have seven pairs of green underwear!" she said. They burst out laughing.

"No, really," she said, trying to stop laughing. Then, after a moment of thought, "I wish that no matter what happens . . . no matter what . . . we'll always be very best friends forever and ever." Stevie paused and then added, "Now you tell me one."

David thought for a second and said, "OK. Since we're gonna be best friends forever, you gotta promise me this. If I die first, you won't forget me . . ."

"David!" Stevie interrupted, flustered. "How could you say that?!"

"Just listen, then promise. You won't forget me and you gotta promise that when I die you won't be sad. I could never leave you. I NEVER will," he promised.

Stevie wasn't sure that he was making sense but he sounded so sincere. She honestly believed him. She was silent for a second. "I promise," she said. "And the same goes for me."

They smiled at each other as they gathered their sleeping gear silently. The sky became radiant as the sun continued to rise. They walked up the hill to Stevie's house, where a steamily delicious breakfast of pancakes awaited them. As Stevie ate, she tried to make some sense out of what David had said.

A few days later, David was supposed to come over and watch the baseball game with her on TV. It had already begun. Stevie began to pace, nervously glancing out her window each time she passed. She tried to sit down and just relax, but couldn't. She knew David would call if something was wrong. This wasn't at all like him. About fifteen minutes later the telephone rang. It was David.

"I'm really, really sorry. I'm calling from the doctor's office. I just forgot to tell you about my appointment. I'm really sorry. Tell me who wins, OK?" He hoped she would not be upset.

"No problem," Stevie said, trying to cover her disappointment. She plopped back down on the couch and gloomily watched the baseball game alone.

"Ready . . . set . . . GO!!" Stevie shouted as they ran through the field toward the finish line two weeks later. Stevie won for the second time in a row against David.

"Come on," Stevie said. "Three out of five!" She was suddenly filled with great confidence from her victories.

"OK," David agreed, panting for air. They began to race again and after a few yards David dropped back tremendously. Stevie stopped in her tracks and turned around to find David hunched over and gasping for air. She had never seen him do such a thing.

"Are you all right?"

"Fine," he replied. "Just out of breath."

Stevie knew David didn't get tired that fast. He could run four or five races before getting winded.

Something was definitely wrong. But Stevie didn't say anything more about it.

Stevie began to see less and less of David, but she worried more and more about him. As the month dragged on, David seemed to grow weaker and weaker. They stopped racing and nearly stopped even seeing each other because David was constantly at doctor appointments. And there were so many of them, one right after another! When Stevie and David were together they would spend their time playing board games and things like that. David, who had always been smiling, smiled much less. Everything used to get a flash of his pearly whites, but not anymore. Stevie watched an enormous transformation take place in David over that month. It was especially sad to see the smiles disappear.

They pretty much kept the problem to themselves until one day when Stevie just couldn't stand it anymore. She decided to take action. As David was returning home from another doctor appointment he found Stevie sitting on his front steps waiting for him. She stood as he approached her and took his arm, steering him in another direction.

"We've gotta talk," she said softly. They walked in silence for quite some time, side by side, their shadows leading the way, before Stevie broke the horrible sound of quiet.

"What is going on?" she said in a frustrated tone. It was clear what she was talking about. When David did not answer, Stevie didn't ask twice. She knew that he would answer when he was ready. He suddenly stopped walking and looked Stevie right in the eye.

"They tell me I have cutis anserina."

"Cute . . . what?"

"Cutis anserina," he repeated.

"What on earth is that?!"

"It's . . . GOOSE BUMPS!!!"

They began to laugh. But Stevie knew it wasn't true. She was glad that he hadn't lost his touch. He could still make her laugh. She loved to laugh with David.

But when she wiped the smile from her face, David knew he had to tell her.

"I have cancer," he said softly. The tone of his voice let Stevie know that this time it was no joke. She desperately searched for some humor in his face but found none. A horrible pang of panic shot through her body like a bolt of lightning. She felt her knees turn to jelly and her jaw dropped. Stevie could feel her heart swimming in her shoes. She felt as if she had just been slapped in the face. "Oh my God" was all she could manage to say.

One day while they were quietly playing a game of Monopoly, Stevie asked David, "Do you ever think about dying?" He rolled the dice and moved his game piece before giving his simple reply.

"Yes."

"A lot?"

"Yes."

"Are you afraid?" Stevie wanted to know.

"Yes."

"Me too," she said softly. She looked at the board to see where David's piece had landed. "You owe me twenty-six dollars rent," she told him in the same gentle tone. They smiled at each other as he handed Stevie the colored paper.

"What do you think will happen to me?" David asked her.

"I wish I knew. Would you visit me?"

"All the time!" His smile was so relieving. They decided that they weren't in the mood to play anymore. Instead, David requested a hug from Stevie. She was glad that they were not afraid to talk about it with each other. So was David.

Three more weeks went by before David was rushed to the hospital. His mother had called and asked Stevie to come immediately at David's request.

As soon as Stevie arrived, she flew to his side. His face was so pale and there were so many tubes hooked up to him and so many machines, it was scary. David looked so sad. She took his hand in hers and fought to hold back her tears, but she no longer could. They rushed down her cheeks as the raindrops had raced down her windowpane. She was petrified. David was going to die, and she was going to sit there watching. A sudden burst of fury shot through her as she realized that the very best friend she'd ever had was dying in front of her and there was nothing she could do to stop it. She could not pretend that it wasn't happening. She clung to David's hand, squeezing harder, as if holding on to him physically could hold him back from dying.

"No," she whispered to the helpless figure on the stiff hospital bed. "I won't let you go!" She gritted her teeth in determination and squeezed his hand even harder.

David said so softly, "Come here." Stevie bent over so that her ear was right by his face. He whispered into her hair, "Stevie, I have to go now. Do you remember when we told secrets in the field? I still promise what I said. I will NEVER leave you."

"I don't understand," Stevie whispered.

"Not in body, but in mind," he continued softly, ". . . in heart . . . in soul. You know how we love the rain. The next time it rains . . . then you will see me. I love you, Stevie . . . I will be seeing you . . . then we'll race for our two . . . out of . . . three . . ."

The tears were streaming down so fast. Her sobs were muffled as she held her free hand tightly over her mouth in disbelief at what was happening. She was crying so hard that she couldn't breathe. Without letting go of his hand she looked up and realized for the first time that David's mom was kneeling at his other side, and his father was standing beside her. To Stevie everything was blurred through her tears. She looked back at David, praying that when she did he would be smiling up at her, saying it was all a mistake.

David opened his eyes and looked at Stevie. He gently squeezed her hand and tried his hardest to smile one last time for her. Then his grip loosened from around her hand and he closed his eyes again.

"NOOOOOOOOO!!" Stevie cried out.

But David could not hear her. The jagged jumping zigzag on the heart monitor had become one horizontal line that ran endlessly across the screen. After a few minutes Stevie carefully laid David's hand at his side, bent over him and ever-so-gently swept a kiss across his cheek.

"Thank you," Stevie whispered. "Nobody could have been a better friend. Nobody . . . " her voice trailed off. David looked so peaceful. She gently pushed his bangs out of his eyes, stood up, and walked out of the room.

The sun had almost completely sunk below the horizon. Stevie stirred on her back porch swing.

Raindrops had fallen from the gray clouds, and a gentle misty fog had settled just above the ground. Stevie wiped her eyes with the back of her hand and looked out over the field. Her field . . . where they'd raced, and told secrets, and laughed. It had belonged to them.

Stevie noticed the raindrops beginning to fall more and more rapidly as they splattered the ground. And all at once, for the first time since David had died three days ago, she smiled. Remembering David's words, Stevie rose from the swing and stepped out into the rain. It was coming down gently and had that wonderful fresh scent. She smiled wider and wider until she began to laugh with joy. The tears on her face mingled with the rain. Stevie was really seeing David, laughing with him! A load of a hundred tons was lifted from her shoulders. She could see him smiling at her for the first time in so long. Stevie cried out to the sky, "I'm so glad that you're here!" and ran down the hill to the field. She ran swiftly, her black dress flapping in the breeze. With a sudden burst of energy she raced three times, then fell exhausted in the wet grass. She hadn't run in such a long time. It felt so good.

"There!" she yelled looking up. "You won! Two out of three!" She smiled and laughed as the rain sprinkled her face. She suddenly felt so strong and free that she could have flown to the horizon in no time at all.

ABOUT THE AUTHOR

Jodi Zislis lives in Columbia, Maryland, where she attends Oakland Hills High School. She has acted since age five, and now is involved in Onstage Productions, a local theater company. She paints, has written several volumes of poetry, and has designed award-winning posters on crime prevention and fair housing. Miss Zislis began writing "It Rained for Stevie" while in the eighth grade at Owen Brown Middle School.

Heroes and Villains

Ambush

by ROGER TSAI

Wake up! Wake up! Come on—move it! Control just called. They're moving right into us. Get into positions!"

My eyes popped open. I grabbed my automatic plasma rifle and quickly crawled into position. It was still pitch dark, save the pale moonlight reflecting off the thick vegetation. We couldn't see them if they were ten feet in front of us, so we had to listen, and be very silent.

This was Ambush Duty, the idea being to try to catch the enemy off guard and blow them away. It always involved hours of sitting in the middle of nowhere in the dead of night, because the enemy didn't stick to the roads and moved at night when our aeroscouts couldn't spot them.

I listened hard. At first there was a lot of clicking and humming, sounds that occur when you pull back the inhibitor switch on a K-12 plasma rifle and let the electromagnets in its barrel charge up. Then I heard our group leader talking with Control.

"Satellite shows fifteen moving straight into your position, Commander, about thirty feet away," said the calm voice of a controller.

"Copy," replied Group Leader. "Listen up," he whispered. "They should be in our faces in a few seconds. Set K-12s to massacre mode, and—good hunting."

I set my K-12 to massacre mode. If the trigger were to be pulled, the K-12 would unleash thousands of rounds of high-energy hydrogen plasma into the night. We all lay there, ready to pull that trigger.

Salty beads of sweat rolled down from my eyebrows and into my wide-open eyes. Every once in a while I moved my hand reluctantly from the trigger to wipe away the sweat. We had heard many tales in which the enemy had turned ambushes into massacres. I had seen troopers die in firefights before, and it wasn't very pretty. When a plasma bolt impacts on a human body, the result is horrifying. The heat and kinetic energy packed into one bolt can punch a hole in a chest, blow off a limb, or sear flesh. Most troopers who took a bolt died immediately, but some died horribly, taking a bolt in the stomach and screaming for hours until they died. It was scary to think of dying that way.

But this was also a time for heroes, a time when boys became men. I was eager to add to the twelve notches on the barrel of my gun, each one representing a confirmed kill. We never found enemy bodies—somehow they always managed to carry off their dead—but every now and then we would find bits and pieces here and there, signifying a confirmed kill.

The enemy was sneaky. Very sneaky.

Suddenly a plasma rifle opened up. Bright flashes of plasma streaked through the night, shedding eerie flickers of light. Then the sounds of more firing rifles, and all hell broke loose, for the enemy had sprung a trap.

Jackhammer-like sounds of discharging plasma rifles filled the air, the sky ablaze with flashes. Plasma bolts hit the ground and trees, pelting me with smoldering bits of dirt and vegetation.

Fear and confusion dominated my mind. I had no idea what to do. It seemed like the enemy was everywhere and I was pinned down, cut off from the rest of my group. The situation seemed entirely insane. I couldn't recognize anything through the haze of smoke and flying debris, and my ability to think was destroyed by the deafening roar of plasma rifles. All I could do was shut my eyes and lie still.

It was very likely that my entire group had already been killed, and I could do nothing. I felt so helpless; I felt like a boy.

I should have gone to college, I thought to myself.

Suddenly, the firing stopped. They probably thought we were all dead. It was pitch dark again, and eerily silent. I decided to try to link up with any survivors, so I crawled as quietly as possible to Benson's position.

Along the way, I called out to Benson in hushed tones, but there was no reply. When I finally reached his position, I saw what had become of him. Benson's dead body lay on its back behind a tree. At first I wasn't really sure it was Benson because part of his face had been singed, but it was. His left shoulder had been completely shot off, and his mouth was wide open in the shape of a scream. He had died most horribly.

I stared long and hard at Benson's mutilated corpse and began to shake with fury. My fear had turned to pure hatred. I would avenge the death of Benson, no matter what the cost.

The enemy would be coming at any time to kill off any survivors of their deadly trap. But this would be the time when I would spring a trap of my own! So I waited.

In a short time, I started to hear slow footsteps. They were very quiet footsteps, probably those of an enemy trying to conceal himself. I looked around and spotted him. He was crouched over, keeping a low profile, and he held a weapon forward, ready to fire on anything that moved. His silhouette slid slowly through the dark.

I raised my K-12 and aimed at him. It was still set on massacre mode, which was more than enough to kill one person. I looked at Benson's eternally frozen face and whispered, "This one's for Benson." Then I pulled hard on the trigger.

I shook violently along with the K-12 as it discharged burst after burst of its deadly plasma into the general vicinity of the enemy soldier. As I let out one long barbaric cry, the shaking stopped and the ammo counter read zero.

The area into which I had fired was leveled of all vegetation, dimly lit by burning trees and shrubs. The body of the enemy lay facedown in the dirt. It was true—vengeance was sweet. I chuckled as I strolled over to the body. I could see that I had done a very thorough job. Several gaping holes riddled the enemy's chest and both of its legs were gone. I bent down and flipped the body over to see its face. I backed off slowly, tripping over my own feet. Then I just sat there in wide-eyed disbelief. This was the enemy?

Two figures ran through the brush and into the clearing. I couldn't have killed them even if I had the ammo. As they approached, I recognized them as the Commander and Sanchez.

"Johnson, you're alive!" the Commander said in surprise. "The enemy has retreated for some reason, I don't know why. They shot us up pretty good."

Sanchez followed with, "Hey look, Commander, Johnson got a kill, body and all. How old do you think he was? Twelve or thirteen? It's hard to tell."

About the Author

Roger Tsai lives in Alexandria, Virginia, where he attends the ninth grade at Thomas Jefferson High School for Science and Technology. Role-playing games, physics, and making artistic paper airplanes are his interests. A "Trekkie," he also enjoys football and wrestling.

A Hard Road Home

by Nathan Costa

Lub-dub, lub-dub . . . I could hear my heart racing . . . *Lub-dub, lub-dub, lub-dub* . . . faster . . . faster . . . My legs, barely touching the ground, were running as fast as I'd ever run in my life. My heart, booming in my ears, thumping so hard, just like it was telling me, "Slow down, Jester! You ain't gonna make it, for you's gonna pass out!"

But I couldn't stop . . . just couldn't. I kept thinking about what Momma said, over and over in my mind, "Jester, if you's gonna run, you gotta do it now! After what you done, they gettin' ready to come an' getcha. You can't stay here . . . shore can't. I'm gonna miss you, but I'm gonna pray to the Good Lord to bring us all back together . . . someplace . . . sometime . . . somehow . . . real soon." Tears rolled down both our cheeks as I held her tight in my arms.

"I'm gonna be back, Momma. You just wait, 'cause I'm gonna be back . . ." And then I ran through the woods by Ol' Man Potter's place and I haven't stopped running since.

With moonlight as my guide, I stumbled over rocks, tree stumps, and roots until I came to a place where I could see that moon rise high above the trees. I looked up and got this real eerie feeling. My chest, still heaving from my run and covered with a sweaty, ripped shirt, felt suddenly cold even though the night was warm. I sat down in the shadow of a tree and asked myself, "Why you runnin' 'way from yer family an' everyone an' everythin' you know, Jester? You don't even know where you goin' 'cept north, an' you can barely fin' yer way!"

I answered myself, "For freedom, that's why!" and started following that North Star in the clear, crisp night. And I told myself, "I won't stop till I git far away from that cotton-pickin' place. I won't stop . . . won't stop . . . won't stop . . ."

"Hey, wake up, kid!" shouted a voice far off somewhere, as my foot was lightly kicked. I moved after the first kick, but then I was kicked again. In my sleep I thought, "Who got the nerve t' do this—kick someone while they's sleepin'? I don't have t'git up! I'm free, an' that's that!" Still, I woke up, feeling like a mouse being watched by an unseen, hungry cat.

"Watcha doin' here, kid? You know you ain't s'posed to be 'round here, doncha?" I was too scared to talk. A white man, about twenty years old, was coming into the moonlight with a shotgun. Was this one o' them that caught slaves an' brung 'em back to their massas for a thrashin'? I asked myself. He was towering over me, about six feet tall—more than a foot taller than me and must of weighed a heap more. His coat with hard shiny buttons on it, all nice and spiffy, was the best piece of clothing I'd ever seen. His being so big scared me so much that when I tried to stand up, I fell back and hit my head on the ground.

He put out his hand to help. "Oh, I see where you been comin' from. You can trust me—I won't tell no one. Honest. You can come with me if you need help." Still scared—because Momma said never to trust most white folks " 'cuz one day they be yo' best frien', then the next day they turn you in like they never seen you 'fore in their life!"—I tried to move away from him and run, but his strong hand held me back.

"C'mon, kid. I'm a friend. I'll help you—I swear." Something, maybe his friendly face and voice, pulled me toward him. I felt better, but I still didn't know his name and wasn't sure I could trust him yet.

"I'm Matt, a soldier in Sherman's army. You know who he is, doncha?" Boy, did I ever! General Sherman was the talk of the plantation back west of Macon. All of us slaves were excited about Sherman and his troops. Folks said he was marching through Tennessee and now Georgia, freeing all the slaves and burning down plantations, buildings, and other things of Southern supporters. We all wanted him to come to us, too, but he never did. We kept hoping and wishing that he'd free us all forever and ever! "C'mon an' I'll git you some food," said Matt.

As we walked through briars and bushes, over tree stumps and logs, I didn't talk much because I was nervous and still scared, but we got acquainted, and I could see he took a liking to me. We silently cut our way through more vines and those mean prickly bushes until we reached a small clearing where I saw burlap tents (with sleeping soldiers in them, I guessed). There were no other soldiers standing around on guard like Matt probably was, and I was thankful for that because I already felt scared enough with just one stranger and most likely couldn't handle more.

We walked alongside the tents quietly, being real quiet beside one tent. "That's Gen'ral Sherman's tent," Matt whispered. "If you wake him, you'll have to reckon with him, 'cause he's real strict, 'specially 'bout gettin' his sleep. He's a light sleeper, an' nothin' gets by him!"

But I wasn't paying much attention to what he was saying, because around the corner were wagons filled with food—bacon, ham, chicken, cornmeal, sweet potatoes, beans, molasses—you name it, it was there! There were even pigs, cows, and other animals grazing next to the food! I'd never seen so much food in all my days! Was this what the North was really like—food for everyone and no one ever going hungry again?

"Eat as much as you want!" said Matt. I couldn't believe it.

"You really mean it?" I asked. No one ever said that to me before! He nodded.

"Well, whatcha want? Take your pick. If you don't mind, I'll have a bit, too, 'cause I haven't eaten in hours." I didn't answer because my head was still spinning from all that food right under my nose. "Here, I'll jest make us some pork, 'taters, beans, an' coffee t' drink. Ever'body likes that 'round here, you too?"

I nodded my head faster 'n you can say "Abe Lincoln." Pork, potatoes, beans, and coffee! I'd never had all those at one meal before! Back at the plantation, we got, at the most, one of those foods at a time, so we were always hungry at Potter's place. We never got enough to get us through the day. But if this was anything like the North was going to be, I'd never go hungry again!

Matt cooked our food. While he did this, neither of us said a word, and I got to take a real good look at him. Matt was very good at his cooking, and if even one little thing was done wrong, he fixed it fast. It seemed like he wanted nothing wrong with our meal.

"Dig in. Hope it's good," he said, handing me a fork and knife. "Jester," he looked me deep in the eyes, "where've you been runnin' from in the first place?"

I had to stop and think. Could I really trust him? Should I tell him anyway? What would happen if he knew and told someone? I'd have to go back to Potter's place? No! Never! But something told me that he wouldn't tell on me. After all, he just made me dinner from wagons filled with all different sorts of food, and he seemed to be a pretty good person.

"I been runnin' away from Potter's plantation near Macon. He used t' beat us real bad when we didn't do nothin' t' him. Seemed that he didn't like nobody but hisself an' his family. We never got 'nough food, 'nough water or clothes, an' he still 'spected us to work like mules in his fields!" I stopped to chew a bite of pork but then started again.

"I 'bout had 'nough o' him an' his spoiled daughters. But when his daughters started teasin' me 'bout my fam'ly, I went and hit 'em upside the head 'cuz I's real mad! They started bawlin' an' howlin' an' cryin' for their papa, so I jus' run off to my momma's cabin. I told her what I done, an' she say I couldn't stay there no more else I'd get hurt real bad. She told me t' run, an' that's what I done. I was runnin' north t' freedom when I met you, an' I best should be goin' on my way once I finish my food. I'm mighty grateful to you, Matt. The meal's mighty good!"

Matt gently put down his fork. "You know, Jester," he began, "if you stay with us, you gonna be free 'cuz we're a Northern army, an' as long as you're with us, you're as free as me!"

I couldn't believe what I was hearing. "Free! Really free?"

"Yup, but only if Gen'ral Sherman 'lows you to stay with us. We always could use some extra soldiers, 'specially those that know the places 'round here. I think I could talk him into it—that is, if you want."

I couldn't hold back my happiness. "Yessuh! Could you really?"

"I don't see why not. But I can't promise nothin'. Don't get your hopes up too high, OK?" But that was all I had to hear. I could be free!—right where I am here in the South—if I stayed with these guys. No massa to whip me, yell at me; no one to take orders from; no one to own me or sell me! I could do whatever I want . . . I could be free!

Matt was already finished eating, but I had barely started. The salt pork cooked over the open-pit fire was juicy and tender. The army must give its best food to these guys here on the warfront! The beans and potatoes went real well with the meat—steamy but not too mushy, just how I liked them. There was no bread like at Potter's, but the food was much better than the leftover slop they fed us at the plantation. Now for the first time in my life, my stomach was fully filled!

"I think I got an extra blanket for you t' sleep on,

if you want—even though you prob'ly hafta sleep outside—if that's all right with you," Matt said as he was
cleaning up. He was cleaning the scraps from his plate
near the edge of the woods. There was no spare water to wash out cups or plates, so he told me to keep
mine close by. By now, it seemed like the middle of
the night, and I was getting really lazy and sleepy, especially from all the running—and eating!—I'd done
that day. When Matt finished cleaning up and dump-
ing dirt on the fire, he went back to guarding the camp.

I didn't like the idea of sleeping outside, but since
I thought it would bring me my freedom, I acted like
it didn't bother me. As I was spreading out my blanket on the ground a little ways from the nearest tent,
I was thinking about what I had done that day—leaving all that I knew for my liberty, how being in that
army was my ticket to freedom, and about my new
friend, Matt, and General Sherman. Looking up at the
stars, I prayed to the Lord that He would guide me to
freedom in the North and that He would help Momma
and all my brothers and sisters keep their patience back
at Potter's. A liberator from the North would save
them and give them their freedom, too. But most important, I asked the Lord to help bring me and my
family back together again when we could all be free.

I hugged myself with the blanket to keep warm,
and in no time, me and my filled-up belly were fast
asleep.

Matt woke me up late the next morning. "Watcha
been doin'? You missed breakfas', an' we're 'bout ready
to git on marchin'! I saved a bit o' food for you in case

you're hungry, but t'morrow you gotta wake up before sunrise. It's almost," he looked up at the sun, "eight o'clock already!" He tossed me a brown haversack. "The food's in there. Ain't much but it'll last you till dinner." Matt started strolling away when he turned around and said, smiling, "Oh, by the way, I gotcha cleared with Gen'ral Sherman. You gonna hafta sleep outside, an' I can't getcha a uniform. He's gonna want t' talk with you 'bout goin' into Macon. But otherwise, you're in, kid!" His mood went back to being serious: "Now let's get a move on!"

I humbly and quietly thanked him. I could see that everyone had gotten up a long time before I had. Tents from last night were all taken down, the campfires sputtering and about to go out. Some soldiers, passing time before marching, were playing cards with torn strips of paper; others were having their last sip of coffee, talking to each other around their campfires, and looking at me as if I didn't fit with them. They were in those blue uniforms just like Matt's, and some were cleaner than others.

I opened my haversack and found some hard, thick crackers, bread, and coffee beans. The crackers were slimy and dirty, but I was used to that kind of thing from living on a plantation all my life.

The coffee was in a small tin can and my cup from the night before was there, too. I started eating my bread when Matt called me over to the one tent that was still left up.

Stuffing the bread as quickly as I could back into my haversack, I dropped the bag and ran to him. A man with messy hair and a frowzy beard and moustache led the conversation.

With Matt standing at attention, he began, "Young boy, as you may've guessed, I am General Sherman, and hereafter you will call me thus. Howard here— you probably call him Matt—has told me about you, Jester. You're a slave from around here, aren't you?"

"Yessuh," I answered, really scared of him.

"And you know your way around these parts, right?" he asked again. I nodded. "We plan to go through Macon today and free slaves like we've been doing all along. Now, Matt and I don't know much about these parts, and I was figuring you could help show us around. Would you like to lead troops with him into the city?"

"Yessuh!"

"Good! I think we can trust him, don't you think, Howard? He seems like a good kid." Matt nodded yes. Then Sherman started barking out orders for the other soldiers.

"Today we will lead three groups into Macon," he said. "McCaine and Jones will lead from the north, Howard and this colored boy," pointing at Matt and me, "will lead from the west. This kid knows the area, and he'll be helping Howard guide his troops. I'll be coming right up the middle with the rest of the men from the northeast towards the city. We'll want to con-verge at the center of the town after doing our stuff along the way. Then we'll go through Griswoldville and Gordon on our way to the sea, but I'll be telling you about that later on. So let's meet in Macon at eleven o'clock sharp. Any questions? Good! Now get your men together and march!"

I felt so proud! General Sherman picked ME to help lead a march with Matt! Wait till Momma hears about this! She'll be so proud o' me for freein' all the

slaves 'round here from their owners! I could feel my
chipped front tooth sitting on my lower lip as I smiled,
and my cheeks felt like they were on fire.

"C'mon, Jester," Matt said. "We got work t' do.
An' wipe that silly grin off your face!" After gathering up our group, Matt told our plan to the soldiers.
When they heard that a thirteen-year-old Negro boy
was leading their march, they snickered and sneered,
but I paid them no mind and held my head high.

Not one of them knew this place better than I did.
I didn't live right in Macon, but I knew that place inside and out—where the mean white folks lived, where
the good ones were, and everything else about the town.
I was sure I knew Macon, and General Sherman knew
that, too.

We got to the outskirts of Macon right before eleven.
All three of Sherman's groups marched into town from
their different directions at the same time! The men
were all loose, making jokes (especially about me being small), and betting on how long the attack was going to take. I was nervous. I didn't know what to expect at all.

Shotgun in my hands, thoughts raced through my
mind. Was there going to be fighting? Would the slave
owners all get together and fight hard against us? Would
the owners be killed or driven out? Would I get hurt?
Die? Before I could even think about it, Matt suddenly
shouted out, "Do your stuff, men!"

The soldiers did as they were told. They ran out
of their two straight lines toward barns, farms, plantations, shops—whatever they saw. Buildings were soon
set on fire; barns, shops, and houses were falling all
around me; arsenals were ripped apart, railroad tracks

were being pulled up.

Men who begged the soldiers to spare their houses and families were shot and killed in the streets. Soldiers ran through houses, stealing jewelry, food, and animals. Before lighting the barns, cattle and horses were pulled out and gathered together. All this happened under the eagle eyes of General William Tecumseh Sherman.

Why were they doing this? Innocent people killed in the streets, crying for mercy. Everyone punished for the wrongs of just a few. There's got to be some reason for this, I thought. There must be, 'cuz look at Matt, my good friend Matt! He's burning and killing, too! But why? Why?

Soldiers, screaming like mad dogs, carried out all the food—or anything worth money—they could get their hands on. And then those places were set on fire, leaving no food, clothing, or even a place to live for those poor folks. Forests were burned, too, and fields. Now the animals had no place to live, either.

Anything that helped the Rebels was burnt, stolen, or destroyed. Bridges and factories became piles of cinders; railroads lost their tracks; all machine and gun-making shops were ruined.

I just stood there, gun at my side, staring. I could hardly breathe. I thought, Must be some reason. Has to be one. No one breaks up towns just 'cuz they in the South! But that's what was happening, right in front of my face. Soldiers laughed at people; they loved taking away their homes, food, clothing, fields, crops, animals. The idea was to leave nothing to rebuild on.

Soldiers were also attacking slaves—burning their houses, taking the little food or anything else they had.

I kept saying, "Why is this happening?" but no one could hear me. I tried to stop Matt, but he was just like the others, charging through houses and fields with his lighted torch, whooping with delight.

Suddenly, a slave woman dropped down to me on her knees. "Please, boy," she pleaded, clawing at my clothes. "Please tell them men over there not t' burn down our cabin. I know massa don't care none for us, but we never did him no harm. Please call them off 'fore they light our house!"

Before I could help, she looked back from her knees at her shack. It was already burning. And those devils were laughing! Laughing at the way she was crying and pleading for mercy! Laughing because she had no more clothes, food, or possessions! Laughing at her family running from the burning shanty, huddled all together not far from where I stood, bawling.

Anger hit me like a hurricane blowing in from the ocean. In my rage I said nothing, but picked up my gun and shot McCaine, the first soldier in blue I saw, straight in his back. I had never fired a shotgun before but had seen them used. The force surprised me and threw me onto my back.

Once they heard my shot, some soldiers dropped their guns and ran toward their lieutenant general. Others just stared at me. With the woman at my feet, still looking up at me from her knees, I did not then realize the seriousness of what I had just done. Then it hit me. I said to myself, "Oh, Lord, Jester, now what have you done?! First you leave everthin' plus your fam'ly to go off somewhur to join this good-fer-nothin' army, an' now you go an' shoot one o' your own off'cers. You can't stay here, same as you couldn't at

Potter's. No, you shore can't stay here 'cuz they gonna getcha and punish you fer shootin' McCaine!"

I couldn't show my face to Matt after what I did. Matt took me in and helped me when I needed him, and all I did to thank him is shoot one of his commanding officers. I shouldn't have even been there! I should've been back at Potter's with all the other slaves, waiting for our freedom peaceably. At least there I'd have my pride and could show my face.

As the soldiers dropped their weapons and torches to go doctor McCaine, I ran off into the woods which I knew so well—faster than I did the first time I was running. I knew some of them would shoot at me, but it couldn't be worse than staying with guys who would punish me just like they punished people for things they did not do. I could never stay with such crazy folks nohow.

A bullet whizzed by my ear. It didn't matter; I ran and didn't feel scared. More bullets were shot, but with each one I kept that funny kind of calm people get when they're really afraid. "It's only little bit 'way, Jester! Keep runnin'! It's gettin' closer! Keep goin'!"

My chest about ready to bust, I ran and jumped over logs, rocks, and roots, through branches, bushes, and leaves. But no one was coming after me. No more shots rang out. No search parties. I finally stopped running near a stream and had some water.

I sat down, resting my back against a tree. "Guess I'll hafta camp out for a few days till they leave fer Griswoldville," I said to God (if He was still listening). "They boun' t' find me if I leave now." My only problem was that I had no food. With all the shooting going on, I had dropped my haversack while I ran.

I hoped they would leave soon and not stay and look for me.

A while later, I heard shots again. People still screaming for soldiers to spare their lives and goods, soldiers laughing their fool heads off. I was fighting with myself: one part of me said, "Watcha doin' here, Jester? People's screamin', dyin', an' cryin' out there, an' you just sittin' here doin' nothin', you low-down, lazy louse!" Another side said more calmly, "Jester, think 'bout it. If you go back, you gonna get yourself killed, or they gonna find you an' do somethin' terrible. You by yourself can't help all them people now 'gainst a whole army. Do it later, once they's all gone." I went along with that second side, even though I felt real bad about all the suffering in the city. But what help could I be?

The one person I did not feel sorry for was McCaine. Yes, he was the first unlucky one I saw when I took up my gun. I could've picked any one of the bunch. I just wanted to prove my point. And I did. I would've done that to anyone who was burning and killing and stealing. So, to be honest, it didn't bother me. It had to be someone.

What were all those soldiers doing here, anyway? I thought they were supposed to be freeing slaves. Now they were going through places and making them unfit for any person—brown or white—to live in. The South would be barren land once Sherman went through it all. What good would it be to the North if everything is useless to everyone? Do they really hate the South that much? I used to think Sherman was the Great Liberator of the Southern Slaves. Ha! Was I sure wrong! I know better now. He's just as bad as the plantation massas. He must hate slaves just like so many of the massas do.

By now it was dusk and everything was quiet. I slowly crept out of the woods and watched as the red-orange ball went down behind the purple hills. I could still smell the ashes and cinders of the fires. Off in the distance I could hear the drumbeat of troops leaving the city. They couldn't have done anything more to Macon; it was burnt to the ground. Still in their razor-straight rows marching to the drum, to them Macon was now history.

I walked slowly out of the forest, heading for the smoldering fires of Macon. Along the way I met a few of the many wounded people. Some limped, had gunshot wounds. Others were burnt, scarred with ash. I built a fire from the wood of a burnt barn to help them keep warm. I ripped pieces from my shirt, and with water soothed the pain of burnt people. I couldn't give them any food, but the people were still grateful to me for my help.

After I'd helped them all I could, I began burying their dead. All of them were strangers, but when I thought about all the pain and hurting they'd gone through, each one seemed like kin. I buried them where they'd fallen, and I said little prayers that my momma taught me when I was just a little boy—too young to know about the hardships of this life—to give them their final resting rites.

As night fell over Macon, I was bone-tired. But before I slept, I again asked the Lord to keep my momma and my brothers and sisters safe from Sherman and his men. I prayed that we would be brought together, and that I would be able to help my family and every other family in Macon build back their lives.

The next morning I walked down the torn-up roads to where I was once a slave. Many other people, coloreds and whites, were carrying their dead loved ones and walking in the opposite direction, trying to get far away from the hell that was their city. They were crying and moaning, with tears running down their faces. I, too, began to cry. "Lord," I prayed, "help us all to OVERCOME!"

Once my last amen was out, I saw Momma! She was going in that opposite direction with the others, all her children, my brothers and sisters, trailing behind, their heads bowed low. My eyes busted out in tears as I ran toward her. I don't think she saw me at first, but when she did, she cried out in a mix of joy and sadness. Slung over her right shoulder was Shawn, my brother, not much younger than me. He was dead. All seven children crowded around and hugged us both, despite Shawn. My prayers had been answered!

We had nothing, but we had everything. Together—and free at last.

ABOUT THE AUTHOR

Nathan Costa lives in Chapel Hill, North Carolina, where he attends Chapel Hill High School. He wrote this story while in the eighth grade at Guy B. Phillips School, also in Chapel Hill. A recent graduate of the North Carolina Boys Choir, he has sung extensively throughout the eastern United States. Basketball is his favorite sport.

Theft

by ELIZABETH WEBSTER

I looked up at Mr. Rodriguez in disbelief.

"D–?" I asked. He fumbled with his marking book.

"Yes, D–." He closed the book and looked up at me. Advice time, I thought. I knew this ritual only too well. He flung the navy book on his mahogany desk and stood up. I'd never noticed how big he was before. "Now, I suggest this to you, young man: Stop cutting class, do your homework and . . . for God's sake, boy," he slammed his hand down on my shoulder, "look at me when I talk to you!" Our eyes met. It wasn't exactly pleasant. His eyebrows were all scrunched together and he looked about ready to howl. Truth was, I felt like picking up the ceramic map of Spain he had on his desk and . . . well, you can imagine what.

I left school that day in one of the worst moods of my entire life. Besides trying to figure out a way of explaining how I managed to get below my usual "D" in Spanish, I had Bradley English, "the momma's boy," walking me home. He lived in one of those rich, three-story houses—you know, the kind with an attic so big you can fit a whole apartment into it.

I looked at my feet. They didn't offer much consolation. I trudged through the snow and ice in my worn-out Nikes. They had little holes all over the place and my feet were becoming painfully numb because the sneakers seemed to be absorbing more water than they were repelling.

I looked over at Brad. He looked like a big fat stuffed animal, wearing tons and tons of woolen articles and a down jacket that must have taken five hundred ducks to stuff. His combat boots clunked against the cement sidewalk and made my feet feel even colder.

I opened my new pack of Newport Lights and lit one up in an attempt to get the jerk off my trail. He hurried after me still. "You know," he began, "you really shouldn't smoke so much. Studies have shown that it can damage your lungs." I kept my eyes glued straight ahead, keeping my mouth shut. I thought to myself: *What I wouldn't do for that ceramic map now!*

"Listen," he continued. "I'm not trying to pester you. I'm simply stating the statistics." He put his hand on my shoulder to slow me down. This was too much. I turned to him.

"*You* listen," I began. "Why doesn't pwecious wittle Bwadley skip on home to his mommy? Hurry along now! She might get worried that her pumpkin got hurt or something . . . and wittle Bwadley wouldn't want his mommy to worry now, would he?" With this I let a mouthful of smoke out into his fat face. I can be pretty nasty sometimes, if I'm in the mood. He coughed for a minute or so, and then let the subject drop. I always knew he was a smart boy.

I turned down Avenue I. Two more blocks to go, I thought to myself. Thank God for that. I glanced around the neighborhood . . . my neighborhood. After last night's snowstorm it had become almost unrecognizable. Thick blankets of snow covered the cars of those smart enough to stay home, and white frost lined the tiny barren branches of trees, making them look glossy and delicate. Besides my numb body, and having to trudge in snow that came way above my ankles, I loved the winter. It made everything so peaceful.

Suddenly a little squirt in a leather jacket tore through me and Brad, ramming my arm into my stomach. The kid knocked Brad down to the cement, where his heavy body landed with a thunk in a large frozen puddle. I looked up. The kid had a pocketbook.

Then I heard the scream. It was from Mrs. Rutherford, the widow who lived in the apartment two doors down from mine.

"Help! Help!" she screeched. "Hoodlum! Hoodlum! Come back here, you—" It didn't take me long to figure out what was going on, and it didn't take Mrs. Rutherford long to realize that Brad and I were the only ones to help. I looked up at her and her eyes pierced my very soul. She turned away.

"Brad! Bradley English! Help! Help!" She never did like me. Nevertheless, I knew that stuffed excuse for a boy wouldn't do anything. I had to do something, whether she trusted me or not.

I dropped my books on Brad and ran after the boy. My sneakers didn't provide the best traction in the world and I was surprised that I didn't go flying into a fence or something.

As soon as Mrs. Rutherford realized that I was the one doing the running, her shrieks became more and more horror-filled. I heard her bang Brad on the head with her umbrella and tell him to get off his "rear" and get her purse. His slow and heavy footsteps followed after me. I could tell he was more than a little reluctant.

The kid I was chasing was pretty small, and finally I caught up with him. He had on a torn brown leather jacket and was wearing sneakers, like me. I could hear him breathing heavily. When I got to within two or three feet of him, I gave a flying leap and landed on the kid's back. We hit some smooth ice and went sliding for about two car-lengths. Finally we stopped moving. I just lay there—on top of his back. I was pretty big for my age and the kid couldn't budge. He began to whimper.

I brought my rough hands up to his neck and picked him up by his torn collar. His face was red and he refused to look me in the eye. I grabbed the pocketbook from his grip. It didn't take much effort—the kid was pretty weak.

Just then Brad came puffing up the block. His warm breath came out in blasts, and huge clouds of white formed before his face. He wobbled over and stood beside me. I couldn't think with him there, as usual. "Here," I said, and slapped the purse into his hand. He looked at me with this confused look on his fat face. For the life of him, he couldn't figure out what to do with it. I slapped him upside his head and shoved him in the direction of Mrs. Rutherford. He nodded and was off, walking slower than my mom drives in the snow.

I turned back to the kid. He just stood there, not even attempting to move. It was as if he almost wanted to be caught. I gripped my hands around his scrawny white neck and put my face in his. He was only nine or ten. His hair was dirty blond, not really knotted or anything, but kind of filthy looking—and feeling. His pale white skin was stained with streaks of black muck or something, and he didn't smell good. No, he didn't smell good at all. He didn't look good at all. He looked like a kid who had no one to look out for him, no one to love him. That made me hesitate before closing my hand harder around his neck. I could empathize with him. But that didn't make what he did right.

I pulled myself together and grasped his head—this no-eye-contact bit was getting to me. With a jerk of the head his eyes met mine. He had glossy gray eyes with a trace of blue in them. But the blue seemed to have been strained out of them, leaving them drab and icy. Icy and so very distant. They looked at me in such a way that I almost let go of him. But I couldn't. I had to say something.

"Now tell me, kid," I began, "what's your name?" He struggled to get away but, as I said, he was pretty weak. He didn't get anywhere.

"I ain't got no name," he spit out. I took hold of his arm.

"Well," I began, "whatever you want to call yourself . . . is this your idea of fun—stealing little old ladies' purses? . . . Huh?" I swung him around and pushed his scrawny body against a blue van. He was really tiny! And he looked so afraid—so pitiful! I tried to appear furious. "Now listen here, kid! How would you like it if I went and told your mom and pop about this little hobby of yours? . . . Hmmm? You wouldn't like it too much, would you?"

He looked down at his frayed jeans and bit his lip. By this time I had stopped pushing him against the van. Now he was just standing there in front of me. All of a sudden he had this funny expression on his face—one that I couldn't quite make out. Finally he spoke.

"I ain't got no old man," he said in barely a whisper, "and no mother either. So take me to the police if ya feel like it, 'cause I could care less!"

My hand loosened its grip around his neck and my fingers didn't push into his jacket so hard. Suddenly I knew why he was so weak! So could he help it if his parents went and died on him? Suddenly I didn't see him as a criminal. I saw him as a little kid who just wanted some spare change for maybe a bite to eat. And I wanted to help.

I stuck my hand into my jacket pocket and pulled out the three bucks I had made last week shoveling walks. I was gonna use them to buy myself a pair of gloves down at the A&P. Oh well, my hands were used to being cold anyway.

I pushed the money into his coat pocket and looked him in the eye.

"Listen, kid—don't go around stealing old ladies' purses . . . or anyone's. Or wallets or watches or jewelry, hear? It ain't right. It just ain't." I patted the money in his tattered pocket. "Now move along and get yourself something to eat at the store. And no candy. Eat some meat or something, got it?"

He looked at me as if he were about to cry and nodded his head. I was probably the first person who had cared for him in years. He straightened up and that caring look faded from his eyes. For someone who has never been loved, it is hard to love. I gulped to hold back what was coming. "Now get lost." I stepped back and watched him tear out of sight, in the direction of "Martha's Deli and Hero Shop."

When he was no more than a tiny speck in the distance, I looked down at the gray pavement. It was rough and uneven, broken to small pieces in places. " . . . unfair," I said aloud, half not hearing my own voice. "Why? . . . why?" For the life of me, I couldn't understand why this poor kid was deprived of his parents and why Brad had . . . well, just about everything. Funny I had never noticed how unfair life was before. I always just accepted that Brad's parents had one of those big, black shiny cars and mine got stuck with a little silver Toyota Tercel with a broken headlight and stolen radio. And everyone liked him, trusted him. Well, what about me? Why didn't they like me? And who was the one to get Mrs. Rutherford's pocket— my thoughts were cut off by the reminder of what had just happened. The pocketbook! I had forgotten all about it. I turned around and started toward 36th Street, where the kid had bumped into me and Brad.

Mrs. Rutherford was standing with her pocketbook in hand and a large grin on her wrinkled face. Her lips rolled back to reveal a ton of gum and two large gold caps. They sparkled under the glare of the sun and somehow gave off a warning signal that said, "Stay away, kid."

I started to think of possible excuses as to how the

kid got away. I couldn't explain what happened—they wouldn't understand. I decided to say he was too quick for me. "You see, Mrs. Rutherford," I would say, "the kid was just too quick for me. Every time I tried to grab him he would slip right out from under me. Oh, well. At least I got you your pocketbook back—that's what really counts." Then she'd smile at me and get all mushy—thanking me left and right—and I would smile back at her and tell her it was nothing, nothing at all. I decided that she wouldn't care much if the kid got away. At least I hoped she wouldn't.

When I was a block away from them, I looked up. Brad was telling some kind of story. As I came closer I could pick up a few of his words. Here's what he was saying:

"You see, Mrs. Rutherford, he was tough, but I could handle him . . ."

I couldn't believe what I was hearing! I really couldn't. He continued.

"Yes, it was dangerous . . . but with my fighting experience it was no trouble at all . . . could've done it with one hand tied behind my back."

He was dishing it out!

"With his fighting experience?" I nearly screamed. The thought of it made me laugh. She couldn't buy it . . . she wouldn't buy it.

Brad saw me coming and gulped. He bent over and lifted his books off the snow-covered cement, never taking his eyes from the sidewalk. I turned to Mrs. Rutherford and cleared my throat. "Um . . . ," I began. "I . . . ah . . . see you've got your pocketbook, ma'am." She turned a cold eye on me.

"It's Mrs. Rutherford to you, young man," she said

abruptly. "And, yes, I did get my pocketbook. Bradley here got it for me." She turned around and looked with kindly eyes upon the stuffed duck.

I was beginning to feel ill . . . and kind of dizzy. I couldn't accept what was happening. I really couldn't. But at least she didn't ask where the kid was. That was something . . . I guess.

"Yes," she continued, "you could do worse than to take a few lessons from this young man." With this, she patted him on the shoulder. I caught a glimpse of his dark brown, almost black eyes. They were kind of glazed and they looked a little scared. He smiled politely and then spoke up.

"Well, ah . . . ma'am," he began. "It was no trouble, no trouble at all." He was backing up the sidewalk. If he didn't watch it he'd fall out over the curb. "No trouble," he repeated. He cleared his throat. "But I'll have to . . . ah . . . get going. Gotta get home. You know how Mother worries when I'm out late—and in the snow? Whew! Would she be upset! Ah . . . yeah, well—bye, Mrs. Rutherford. Bye, um . . . ." He looked up at me. "Bye." The coward couldn't even say my name. I looked into his ruddy face. My eyes hit his and I must have been giving him the dirtiest look ever, 'cause he just turned around and practically raced up the street—almost got hit by a station wagon crossing Brooklyn Avenue.

By this time I had given up. Everyone always thought I was a loser . . . why should now be any different? It wasn't. It would never be different.

Out of nowhere it began to flurry. I really didn't understand that—it was sunny a minute ago. The cold flakes fell on my nose and my numb fingers and reminded me again of how cold I was—just what I needed.

Mrs. Rutherford looked over at me. "What's the matter with you, boy?" she said. "Where are your gloves . . . and your hat?" Her eyebrows slowly lowered. "For God's sake, doesn't your mother take care of you?"

That stung like hell. I kept my eyes on the ground, staring, going over the tiny cracks in the pavement. I had never noticed how badly the sidewalks around here needed repair. Mrs. Rutherford just stood there, probably staring at me. People are always staring at me for one reason or another.

"Well, boy," she continued, "thanks for helping Bradley get my pocketbook. I'll be on my way now." She stood there. She must have expected me to respond with a "you're welcome" or even a simple "goodbye," but I just didn't feel like saying anything. She'd have to wait there all day and night if she wanted something outta me. She mumbled something I didn't quite catch and was finally on her way.

It began to snow harder, and my ears and cheeks felt as if they really weren't on my face. I kept biting my lip and I had this funny feeling in my throat—kind of like I was about to cry. I had to bite it harder and harder to keep it all inside, but I couldn't. I guess I had just had enough. I didn't realize how hard I was biting my lip until I felt the warm blood stream into my mouth. My lip began to sting and my teeth lifted up from it. As I did this, one teardrop rolled out of the corner of my eye and plopped down on the broken pavement below. It fell between one of the larger cracks and the soil soaked it right up.

ABOUT THE AUTHOR

Elizabeth Webster lives in Brooklyn, New York, where she attends Polytechnic Preparatory Country Day School. She wrote this story in the eighth grade. Besides writing, her interests include singing, acting, playing the piano, and animals. She takes care of six cats, some birds, and two dogs.

Story Index

By genre, topic, and for use as writing models

By Genre

Fantasy

Historical Fiction

Realistic Fiction

Science Fiction

By Topic

Alienation/Outcasts

Animals and Nature

Coming of Age

Family

Friendship

Life and Death

Prejudice

Self-image

War

As Writing Models